Untethered Magic

Steve Higgs

Text Copyright © 2020 Steven J Higgs

Publisher: Steve Higgs

The right of Steve Higgs to be identified as author of the Work has been asserted by him in accordance with the Copyright, Designs and Patents Act 1988

All rights reserved.

The book is copyright material and must not be copied, reproduced, transferred, distributed, leased, licensed or publicly performed or used in any way except as specifically permitted in writing by the publishers, as allowed under the terms and conditions under which it was purchased or as strictly permitted by applicable copyright law. Any unauthorised distribution or use of this text may be a direct infringement of the author's and publisher's rights and those responsible may be liable in law accordingly.

'Untethered Magic' is a work of fiction. Names, characters, businesses, organisations, places, events and incidents either are the product of the author's imagination or are used fictitiously. Any resemblance to actual persons, living, dead or undead, events or locations is entirely coincidental.

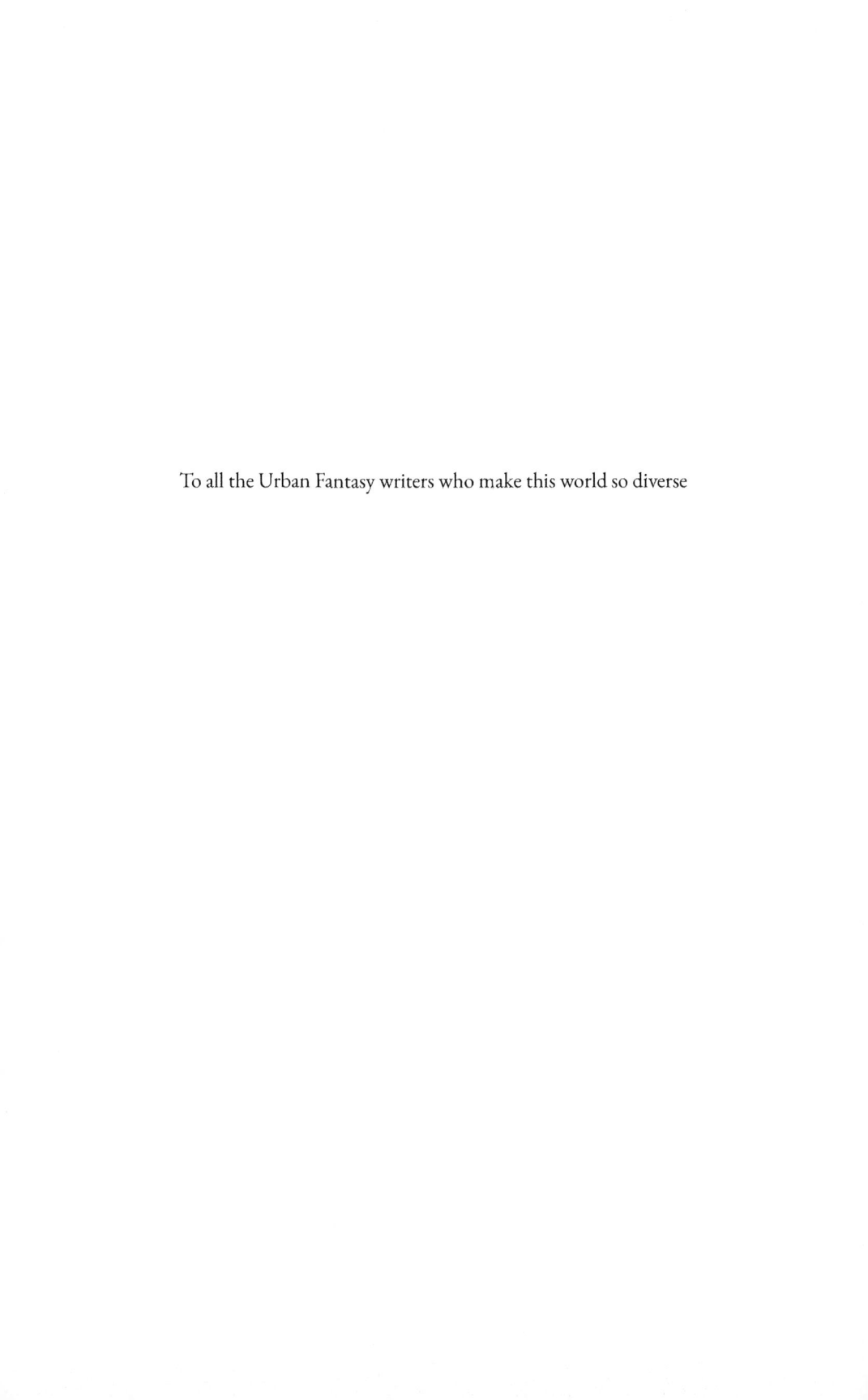

To all the Urban Fantasy writers who make this world so diverse

Contents

1. Chapter 1 — 1
2. Chapter 2 — 7
3. Chapter 3 — 12
4. Chapter 4 — 22
5. Chapter 5 — 31
6. Chapter 6 — 38
7. Chapter 7 — 43
8. Chapter 8 — 51
9. Chapter 9 — 56
10. Chapter 10 — 62
11. Chapter 11 — 66
12. Chapter 12 — 73
13. Chapter 13 — 80
14. Chapter 14 — 85
15. Chapter 15 — 95
16. Chapter 16 — 101
17. Chapter 17 — 112
18. Chapter 18 — 117

19.	Chapter 19	119
20.	Chapter 20	125
21.	Chapter 21	130
22.	Chapter 22	134
23.	Chapter 23	140
24.	Chapter 24	148
25.	Chapter 25	157
26.	Chapter 26	167
27.	Chapter 27	172
28.	Chapter 28	176
29.	Epilogue: The Shifter	180
30.	Author Note:	182
31.	More Books by Steve Higgs	184
	About the Author	185

Chapter 1
January 2012, Bremen, Germany

The streets were almost deserted, even though it was mid-evening; the cold was keeping people indoors. Snow would come soon, everyone expected it and its arrival would warm the city up a little as well as make it look spectacular. The clear sky above let me know the snow wasn't coming tonight though and I shivered for the thousandth time as I cursed myself for not wearing another layer.

I was close to the harbour part of Bremen, a rough area but one I wasn't surprised to find myself in. I was tracking a missing person; a twenty-three-year-old man called David Beckermann who disappeared after a night out eight days ago. It hadn't taken me that long to find him, less than two hours, in fact, since the family contacted me. I was closing in on where I would find him and starting to get a very bad feeling.

My broken compass, the one I developed specifically to channel my tracking spell through, led me into a small delivery area behind a row of businesses where I knew I was about to find his body. Sure enough, less than a minute later, I found the poor man under a pile of rubbish behind a dumpster.

Being careful not to disturb the scene, I shifted a frozen cardboard box away from his face. I already knew it was him for certain; that's how the spell works, but I wanted to see his face to match it to the picture they showed me anyway. Had I not done so I wouldn't have seen the puckered mark on his neck. I studied it, twisting my head this way and that as I tried to work out what I was seeing. I took a picture with my phone for comparison later, my brain categorising it as looking as if something had bitten him, but not with teeth. It looked more like something had pulled or sucked at the skin.

I needed to call the police, and I needed to return to the family home to tell them their eldest son was dead. I could have saved them a week of anguish if they had called me when he first went missing. Not that the outcome would have been any different. The police could have called me too; they have my number, but despite my successes finding missing people, often still alive, the police treat me like something they don't want to touch.

I stood up to make the call to them anyway. There was a body in the street, and the authorities needed to deal with it. He wasn't the only victim recently. There had been too many, in fact. A regular spree if you want to give it a term. I hadn't seen any of the others, but they were in the papers and on the TV, their faces in life far easier to look at than the one I saw in death.

As the call connected and a feminine voice spoke into my ear, I saw something. I had my second sight in place, as I often did when I was tracking or spell casting, which meant I caught a glowing magical aura as a figure went by on the other side of the buildings. The voice on the phone repeated itself, but I thumbed the button to end the call and started after what I had seen.

When I came back out into the street, it was in front of me and moving away, walking along the pavement. It wasn't human, but it was disguised as one. Had I not been looking through my second sight, I might never have noticed it. I closed my eyes and reopened them with my standard vision. Now all I could see was a guy out for a walk. I blinked again, an action that aided me in bringing up my second sight. It went over my vision like an additional filter, showing me things I couldn't normally see and was fairly certain no one else ever saw. Right now, it enabled me to see the creature's true form behind the enchantment it wore.

Not only could I see it, but I could also see that it was about to attack a person. From the sheath inside my left sleeve, I drew out my wand, and with a whispered word, 'Cordus,' I activated my defensive amulet. I had invoked it as usual just before I left the house, the spell using my blood to connect the amulet with my aura, which, once activated, gave me an invisible shield of magical energy that was strong enough to deflect fists, feet and even weapons. However, I wasn't sure what protection it would give tonight because I had no idea what I was about to face.

'Hey!' My shout got its attention.

Further down the street, a face turned my way, that of a young man, a low end of the scale prostitute perhaps, waiting in the cold because his pimp insisted. Without the ability to see through the enchantment that hid the creature's true features, all he could see was a man coming toward him. The prostitute was alert enough to sense trouble, glancing at me and the *man* approaching him before deciding to be elsewhere.

As the young man scurried away, the creature turned its attention to me. Its head swung back to observe the intended prey flee, then shrugged and started toward me instead. I guess it decided one victim was the same as another.

With my second sight in place, what I could see had no hair on its head or face, and its teeth had a triangular shape, much like a shark's, only smaller. Its nose didn't protrude from its face, but was part of it, almost like a snake; two holes could be seen where the nostrils should be. It was able to disguise itself as a man in his thirties with short hair and a bit of stubble, the illusion some kind of enchantment or spell but the clothing was the same using either version of my eyesight; jeans, high-top sneakers and a ski jacket. I saw all that and filed it away in under a second. Speed was essential because the creature was coming straight for me.

I had no idea what it was, but I was willing to bet I had just found the creature that left the puckered mark on my missing person. There was a supernatural creature in Bremen, and its overt hostility made me sure it was the killer the police were searching for.

Flourishing my wand as a warning, I challenged him as he approached. 'Stay there. I am quite able to put you on your ass.' In response, I got a grin like I had said something funny. I wanted to find out more about him. I wanted to know what he was. However, he seemed disinclined to converse and hadn't slowed his approach. If anything, he was picking up speed and about to break into a run.

Drawing energy into my body from a ley line in the earth beneath my feet, I manipulated the air, creating a wall of it to shove the creature backwards. As his feet skipped over the surface of the street and he fought to stay upright, his face registered shock; clearly, he hadn't expected resistance from me. He circled right, looking for an opening. He was hostile, that much was clear, but I couldn't tell if he could talk or not because he was making no attempt to do so.

'Can you understand me?' I asked, watching his face to see how he reacted.

He reached behind his back to produce a short sword, which to me looked like a shiny, black, half-length katana. Light from the moon or the streetlights caught on its edge as he moved it, giving the impression it was scalpel-sharp.

'You are human?' he asked.

Caught momentarily off guard as he brandished his weapon, I answered with another spell, this time conjuring a lance of fire, which I always found hard to control. I only used it now because we were not close to anything flammable.

The creature caught it with the blade, which somehow absorbed the flame, and he continued to study me curiously. Dancing light from the flame distorted his features further, making him more hideous to look at if such a thing were possible. I watched as he sniffed the air, shutting off the lance of flame as worry started to spike my pulse.

'You *are* human,' he decided. 'But with some skills. You may be of value.'

'Value?' I echoed his word, my reaction an automatic response to his statement. I wanted to know more about him, since, at this stage, I didn't even know what he was. 'What are you?' I demanded. 'What are you here for?' I felt certain he was the creature responsible for the recent spree of deaths. His close proximity to a recent victim, a wound I couldn't explain, and his supernatural nature were too much of a coincidence for me to dismiss. 'Were you going to hurt that man?' I asked.

He didn't answer. Instead, he broke into a run and charged me, the short sword held in his right hand as he closed the distance between us. I put my left foot back for balance and drew more power in from the ley line as I moved my protective shield in front of my body.

The ugly beast ran straight into it, thumping against the invisible wall as if running into a thick sheet of Perspex. There was a moment when his face was flattened against the shield, and then he bounced off, losing his balance as he tumbled away, and I hit him again with another lance of flame, this time striking home to wound.

My aim was off, the creature difficult to hit as he rolled across the street, but I tagged his leg, setting his trousers on fire. I followed, maintaining the flame as I tried to inflict more damage, but he rolled to his feet, springing up to a standing defensive position even as the flames licked at his jeans.

With the blade facing me again, he was able to intercept my spell and once again diffuse it. I had a temporary advantage though, my attacks pushing him into a defensive posture, so I pressed on, trying to make it more permanent. Dropping the flame spell, I whipped my arms around to send a blast of dust and dirt his way. My opponent staggered back, flailing his arms to shield his face and giving me the opportunity to go for the big one.

I had to build the pressure this time, feeling out with my senses to generate static electricity in the air around me. Using my wand to continue the barrage of muck-filled air, I was able to keep the creature away from me, while simultaneously using my left hand to weave the charge-filled air into something meaningful.

The creature bellowed in rage, slashing at the air with his blade and cursing in some ancient language. I had him, though; I was winning. The pressure in the air around me was almost enough to use. Just a few more seconds; there was no sense in letting rip until I felt confident it had the power required. I was going to hit him with lightning. I need to point out that until tonight I have never tried to hit anything with it. I can create it easily enough, the spell merely requiring that I agitate the moisture molecules to create the friction which causes the static electricity. I felt confident it would put him on his backside but not kill him, which was my intention. I wanted to ask questions.

The siren caught us both by surprise. As I jumped in shock, the buffeting wind I was using to keep the creature in place dropped for a moment. Our eyes met, and I got what I thought was a grin. Then the air behind him shimmered as he did something with its left hand, and he stepped backward into it and vanished.

I stared at where he had been, blinking and stunned, my mouth opening and closing as I tried to comprehend what had just happened. I had seen the same thing once before and had been searching for the man that I saw do it ever since.

The street was empty. Or, rather, the street no longer contained my opponent. I was still here though and so was the cop car.

As it screeched to a stop ten metres away and the two men inside bailed out with the weapons drawn, I knew I was in for a boring night. At least I would get to warm up.

Chapter 2

I found myself in a bland interrogation room. I had been in here for over an hour already, sitting opposite Detective Sergeant Schenk who was asking me the same set of questions he had been since we sat down. Every few minutes he tried to ask them in a new way. I ran my hand over my dark hair and noticed the bags under my blue-green eyes as I looked in the two-way mirror. I frowned at my reflection, noting that my hairline was continuing to recede. It was beginning to form a widow's peak which was more prominent because I kept my hair cut close to my skull. I am tall, at around one metre ninety, and lean. Others might say thin, but I prefer a term that does make me sound like I need to be fed.

Otto,' Schenk liked to address me by my first name, 'what is this?' The detective's question brought me back from examining my depressingly ordinary features. The overweight detective sergeant held up one of the items they confiscated. He had it in both hands, turning it over and over as he inspected it. A moment ago, he had been asking me what I was doing out and in a dingy part of Bremen at night by myself. The cops in the squad car had spotted me, decided I looked suspicious and arrested me just in case because they had a serial killer on the loose. I had been spellcasting when they arrived, so they must have seen me waving my arms around.

He continued to turn the object over, inspecting it as he waited for me to feel the need to fill the void his silence left.

I wanted to tell him it was a wand. That is, essentially, what I used it for. It was a thin rod of willow about twenty centimetres long. There were no markings on it. There was nothing remarkable about it at all, but years ago, when I had been trying to work out what I could and could not do, I wanted something that I could channel through. The magic, I might as well call it that, which I can conjure, comes from ley lines in the earth. My second sight allows me to see them, and having worked out that I was drawing on those and that was where my magic came from, I devised, through much experimentation, the wand the detective sergeant now held.

DS Schenk brought his eyes back up to look at my face. 'The desk sergeant who booked you in said it was taken from inside your sleeve. Is this part of some odd ritual you perform when you kill your victims?'

'I haven't killed anyone.' It was not the first time I had made that claim in the last couple of hours. 'I already told you I was hired by the Beckermann family to find their missing son. That's why I was out tonight. Have you called them to corroborate my story?'

'Story?' He smiled. 'An interesting choice of words. Makes it sound like even you think it is fiction. Tell me how it is that you were able to find their son's body in just a couple of hours when the police have been looking for over a week. Is it because you knew where you had left it?'

'I find missing people. My success rate in this field is well documented.'

'That wasn't an answer,' he pointed out. He was surly and unpleasant. Perhaps it was something he put on for this part of his job, but I thought it more likely he was just an unpleasant person. His gut was pressing against the edge of the table, though he paid it no attention, which meant he had grown used to it. He had a crumb hanging from his mustache which I couldn't take my eyes off. It was clinging precariously, moving each time he spoke, but it refused to drop. 'How did you find him so quickly?'

'I have a skill that I cannot explain to you.' I learned in the past that there was no point in ever introducing the concept of magic. When you say something like that, it stays with you. People don't forget, and I had to wonder if he was waiting for me to use the word now.

He snorted lightly in amusement. 'Go on, you can tell me. I'm a policeman.'

UNTETHERED MAGIC

I didn't bother to respond.

Schenk twirled my wand in his fingers again, looking down at it before bringing his eyes back up to me. 'The officers who arrested you said they saw you in the street acting in a threatening manner and attacking someone. Why don't you tell me about who you were attacking? What happened to that person?'

'What person? I thought the officers searched the area and couldn't find anyone?' I knew it to be true because I had been handcuffed in the back of their squad car at the time.

'Nevertheless, they saw someone in the street with you. Where did they go?' It occurred to me, while I thought about how to answer his question, that a legal representative might have been able to wrap this up some time ago. However, I had waived the right to counsel the moment it was offered; I didn't want to explain my activities to a lawyer. They would expect me to tell the truth, and I couldn't do that. Not without risking some kind of psychiatric evaluation.

Schenk held up the wand again. 'The victims all have a weird mark on their necks. How do you make it? Is this something to do with it?'

'We are going to keep going around and around, aren't we, Detective Sergeant Schenk? I haven't hurt anyone, and soon you will correlate my movements with previous attacks and be able to show that my whereabouts were accounted for. I told you this more than an hour ago. Can we move it along?'

Schenk cut his eyes at me. He looked like he wanted to hit me, and with no lawyer present, I wondered if he might. 'Think you're smart, do you, Otto? I know you are involved in the death of David Beckermann. You're going to tell me why you killed him and how. Until you do, you're not going anywhere.' I was trying to keep my anger and frustration in check despite the irritating man's desire to rile me. It felt like a tactic on his part, a deliberate attempt to push me into saying something I didn't want to say.

But here's a thing about me; I can tell when a person is lying. It was something I discovered as a teenager. Something about the sound of the words told me when they were not true, and Schenk was lying to me now.

'That's a lie, Schenk. You don't know any such thing. You are holding me because you want to and because you have no other leads. Apart from making me late for my hospital visit, you are just wasting your own time.'

He looked down at his notes, flicking them with the fingers of his left hand while he idly twirled my wand in his right. 'Oh, yes. Your wife, Kerstin, is in a coma, and you visit her every night between nine and midnight.' He frowned at me, his face filled with doubt at the truth of my claim. 'Three hours? Isn't that rather a long time to spend with an unresponsive person every night?' He was goading me. 'She is unresponsive; that's what you said. In a coma for nine months now. How exactly did that happen?'

I had already told him the lie. The same lie I told at the time and would continuing telling forevermore. I came home and found her like it. The lie was easy to tell because it was based on the truth. I had arrived home and found her unconscious. The part I left out was the man I disturbed in our house.

Across the kitchen, as the flowers I brought home for her tumbled from my hand, the man had tipped me a quick salute and stepped backwards through a pool of shimmering air. He was young and handsome, plus athletic in a muscular way, just the sort of man you don't want to come home and find your wife with. When I recovered from the shock of first seeing him and then seeing him vanish before my eyes, I rushed to my Kerstin's side. She was face down on the kitchen tile, her long blonde hair matted with fresh red blood, and she was unconscious. There was a wound to her skull, from a fall, they said. A blow, most likely, had caused bleeding and swelling of her brain. She might yet come around. She might not. They just didn't know.

So, yes, I went to see her every night. My wife of seven years. A tear came with the memory of her smile. I swiped at it and decided I was done answering questions. 'Take me back to my cell. This interview is over.'

Schenk laughed at me, a scoffing noise that suggested it would be over when he decided and not before. Thirty minutes later, when I hadn't said another word, he gave up.

An officer escorted me back to a cell.

Presently I slept.

Chapter 3

When I was finally released without charge six hours later, Detective Sergeant Schenk had long since gone home. They gave me back my belongings, including the wand, but I got a cautionary word before I left, the station chief choosing to invite me into a meeting room himself.

Chief of Police Frans Muller was a man I had met before and dealt with several times. On the first occasion, most of ten years ago, he was still a lieutenant. He was in his late fifties if his face was a reliable indicator, but he hadn't looked after himself any more than DS Schenk had, his beer belly protruding over his belt in much the same way. He was completely bald and clean-shaven, yet had an abundance of hair coming from each nostril and ear as if trying to compensate. His sleeves were rolled up, though the left was rolled one more time than the right which gave him a lopsided appearance. I tried not to look as it made my fastidious nature twitch.

In the meeting room, the chief closed the door and turned to face me. 'Herr Schneider, this is just an informal chat, you understand. Nothing is being recorded, and you are free to leave if you choose to do so.'

My foot twitched toward the door, but I held myself in place to hear what he had to say. 'Go on.'

'We have no evidence of wrongdoing on your part, but I want to stress that I consider your presence on Osterdeich Strasse to be suspicious.' He raised a hand to stop me speaking just as I was drawing in breath to argue. They hadn't found anything to charge me with, so why was he still questioning what I was doing there? 'I don't think you are the killer we are after. I have been a cop for over thirty years, and one gets a feel for different types of people. However, I think you were there looking for the killer.' Again, he raised his hand to stop me speaking. 'I am not accusing you of anything, Herr Schneider. I want, though, to impart a simple piece of advice about vigilantism: it is not a safe thing to do. I know you were there to find the body of David Beckermann. His family have confirmed they hired you, and of course, his body was exactly where you told my officers they would find it. I have to agree with Detective Sergeant Schenk's point about you finding it so swiftly.'

'It's what I do,' I pointed out.

Again he raised a hand to beg me to let him continue. 'Herr Schneider, I remember the rumours about you. Magic and whatnot. I don't know how you do what you do, but the reason for this little chat has nothing to do with any of that.'

'No?'

'The report from my officers makes it sound like they saw you fighting someone. Were you?'

I tussled with what to tell him. If I told him that I believed I had found the killer, he would have me back in an interview room for the next dozen hours. They would want to know why I believed he was the killer, which would instantly put me on rocky ground because I could only explain it by referencing magic. Furthermore, they wouldn't be able to see what I had seen, so my information would just be misleading. Glad that no one else had my ability to hear lies, that's exactly what I did. 'I cannot explain what they saw. When they stopped me, I was trying to call the police to tell them where I found the body.'

The chief squinted at me. 'Yes, we confirmed you made the call, but the call and the arrest were five minutes apart. How do you account for the time difference, Herr Schneider?'

I stuck out my bottom lip in a *what-can-I-tell-you* expression. 'Your equipment is faulty.'

The chief sighed. 'I think you were fighting someone, and I think you were out there trying to find whoever is guilty of the current spree of killings. I beg you, take fair warning. Often as not, the criminal gets the vigilante, not the other way around. And when the vigilante wins, the cops arrest them anyway. But you're a licensed detective, so you know this already.'

'I was just there to find David Beckermann's body.'

'Just be careful, Herr Schneider. I would hate to find you falling victim of your own good intentions. There were two more victims last night while you were locked up here.'

Two more dead. The creature I faced down and almost beat had struck again after he escaped me. Meeting him had been pure luck, the result of coincidence and nothing else. 'I can help you, you know.' I blurted the statement as we were coming back out of the meeting room. My words drew the attention of every cop in the room. There were seven of them, all looking my way now as their chief raised his eyebrows.

'How is it that you can help us, Herr Schneider? What is it that you think you know that you haven't told us?' He was offering me an opportunity to talk about my *special* skills. Not because he believed me, but because doing so would make it easy for him to dismiss me.

I huffed out a breath and went for broke. Choosing my words carefully, I said, 'The victims all have a strange mark on their necks, don't they?' The chief stared at me; his expression unreadable. 'They are dead, but you don't know what they died of.' I was guessing that part, but I could tell I had it right from the very brief look of surprise that flickered in his eyes. He quashed it instantly, but not fast enough. 'Do you believe in the supernatural?' I asked. I knew it went against a principle I had employed for years; talking about magic and the supernatural just opened me up to abuse. However, I felt certain they were dealing with a creature they couldn't comprehend or hope to catch, not when it could vanish at will, so I was placing myself on the bench and would wait until the chief realised he needed me on the field.

A smirk arrived on Chief Muller's face without being invited. He couldn't help it, and I knew this was the response I would get. 'Do you?' he asked.

Ignoring his question, I fixed him with a serious look. 'When you cannot solve this, or you begin to accept that you are not dealing with a man, call me. I won't even charge you.'

This time the chief laughed. 'You won't charge us? That is mightily generous of you, Herr Schneider.' He took my card when I offered it, still smirking at me as he began tapping it on the knuckles of his left hand. He was waiting to see if I had any more to say.

I didn't.

The cops didn't offer me a ride home or back to my car, where I had parked it the previous evening. I found it with a parking ticket stuck to the windshield, the zone having gone live at nine o'clock.

Swearing under my breath, I slid inside and turned on the engine, then turned on the heat and then the heated seat and finally the heated steering wheel. I was cold.

Not for long, though.

My wife was a divorce attorney at one of the big firms in town. She made partner a year ago and had already been scoring what I thought were big bucks before that. Our house was paid for; we could have moved somewhere bigger or swankier, but we hoped for children, though they had proven elusive thus far. To add to the income that came from her job, her firm had a health policy that was covering all her medical bills, and she had a critical illness insurance policy I wasn't even aware of. A woman turned up on the doorstep one day a week or so after my wife's *accident*. She had a fat cheque for me. It was ours even if Kerstin recovered.

When they took her into hospital, I was working a missing persons case. It took me three days to find the person, the sixteen-year-old daughter of a wealthy couple who believed she had been kidnapped. She hadn't. She had run away with a man in his late twenties who believed her claim to be twenty-two. Three days was the longest it had ever taken me to find someone; Kerstin going into hospital distracted me. The sixteen-year-old was pregnant by the time I tracked her down, and her parents offered to sue me instead of paying me. I waived the bill and walked away.

Licensed detective work let me use the skills that... people say the skills that God gave them, but I don't think these came from God. I don't know where they came from, of course, but God seemed unlikely. I tried a bunch of other careers first, settling on this one when a missing persons case in the papers offered a reward to anyone who could provide information leading to the person, a child, being found. I knocked on their door, only twenty-two at the time, borrowed an item of clothing and found their thirteen-year-old son the same day. He was still alive, I got paid, and I saw an opportunity. Soon after that, I was hired for another case, private detective work looking into fraud inside a firm. The case brought me into close contact with an alluring woman. Her name was Kerstin, and I somehow convinced her to marry me.

The house still felt very empty without her. A friend had suggested I get a cat. I would rather pour vinegar up my nose.

I fixed myself some breakfast, a fast and easy plate of ham and cheese with fruit and yoghurt and sat down to consider what I needed to do next. The latest victims from last night took the murder toll to seventeen over a four-week period. Many of the victims were homeless people, the papers initially suggesting it was someone trying to clean up the streets. They changed their minds when a heart surgeon, his wife, and their child were found dead in an alleyway.

Each victim was left with a mark on their necks, according to Schenk. I wasn't sure he intended to give away that little snippet, but he had. It linked David Beckermann to all the other victims, but all I had time for last night was a brief glance. I needed to get a better look. His body would be at the morgue, so now I had to find an excuse for me to be in there. I had no client driving me to catch the killer; however you could argue that with my particular skills, I was the only person in the city who could stop him. I didn't know if that was true or not, but I suspected no one else could see him; everyone else would see the enchantment that made him look like a person.

I wasn't being selfless though. My motivation wasn't to save the people of Bremen. That thought was in my head, but ultimately, my goal was to find the man I saw in my kitchen with Kerstin the night she was hurt. He had something to do with her condition; he had to. Seeing the creature last night using the exact same shimmering pool of air to escape meant they were somehow linked. I would find the creature, then go through him to get to the one I really wanted. Maybe then I would find a way to get my Kerstin back.

I showered and dressed, the effect making me feel refreshed even though I badly needed more sleep. Most of my work is done at night; that's just how my job works out, so I often sleep during the day. I have done for years. I figure it is no different from being a shift worker; there are plenty of people that work at night. My job used to be lots of missing people or private investigator work where I was paid to follow someone's wife because her husband believed she was having an affair. Sometimes they were, and a few photographs were all I needed to get paid. It was slightly sleazy work, but it went with the territory.

Recently, the last five years or so, the nature of the work had got darker. More of the missing persons cases led me to bodies than just runaways. Worse yet, there were some that I couldn't find at all. When I look for someone, my compass instantly gives me their direction. It makes it easy, but it doesn't tell me whether they are dead or alive; I don't find that out until I find them. Over the last couple of years, I have been setting my tracking spell full of confidence, only to find it spins and never stops, unable to locate the missing person. It will find a body buried in the ground, so to just spin tells me one thing: they are no longer on Earth.

Missing people who were not on Earth was one thing, but the number of calls from people who said they had seen something or felt something and wanted me to look into what it was increased too. Bremen is a medium-sized city, but there is only one other registered private detective. I suppose that when the police won't look at your case, which they always refuse to do when it is just something weird with no attached crime, your only option is to take it to someone else. That was going to be me at least fifty percent of the time. Sometimes there was an explanation for what a person had seen, but increasingly more often now, there wasn't. Or, rather, there wasn't one I could give them because I got the sense that they had come across something supernatural.

I thought all this as I went out to my car, a shiny new dark grey Audi A8, a treat from my wife last Christmas. I didn't need to look up where the morgue was, I already knew from a few occasions when my missing person search ended when I found the person was already there and waiting for identification; missing because they were the victim of a terrible crime.

The traffic across the city at this time of day was light, the morning rush to work long done. It meant though, that I got there so quickly I still hadn't worked out what lie I was going to tell. With nothing else for it, I left my car in a slot in the car park and went to the front doors.

'Good morning,' said a man in his early thirties. He was sitting behind a reception desk looking official in a suit and tie, a plastic badge hanging around his neck on a lanyard told me his name was Gustav Henkel. 'Are you with the others?'

I didn't know which others he was referring to, but I said, 'Yes,' and made it sound as natural and convincing as I could.

'Just sign in and I'll buzz you through,' he offered, wafting his biro in the direction of an open visitor's book on the raised part of the reception desk. I couldn't tell if he was new to the job or hadn't been trained or just didn't care, but his lax attitude was going to get me inside.

Seconds later, I was through the door and into the morgue. It was a little early for jubilation though; I hadn't achieved anything yet.

There were voices ahead, several of them, both men and women mixed in together. It presented me with a dilemma. I didn't want to skulk around and look like I was being furtive, but I also didn't want to run into anyone and answer questions about who I was and why I was there. As I drove here, the idea in my head was straight from a film or a television show where I could wander into the morgue room with all the long drawers, find myself alone and pull the drawers out until I found the one I wanted. Quite why I imagined it would be that easy, I had no idea because the morgue was always busy whenever I visited in the past. Regardless of that, having come here expressly to inspect the wounds on David Beckermann, I wasn't planning to leave until I had at least tried. I didn't get very far.

Around the first corner, my stride purposeful as I chose to act like a belonged in the hope others would assume I did, I ran straight into Chief Muller. It took him about half a second to recognise me, the flare of his eyes making my stride falter, and that was my big mistake: it made me look like I was going to try to run.

His order to, 'Stop him,' caused two younger men in police uniform to dart forward. I didn't get the chance to decide what I was going to do because they bundled me up against a wall and pinned me there, my hands behind my back.

I could have done several things to stop them and could do other things now to ensure they let me go. I did none of them though because, for a start, they were police officers, and they would find something to charge me with if I caused them any harm at all, and secondly, I doubted the people in the room were ready to see what I could do.

'I am not resisting,' I announced calmly. 'I am still trying to help.'

'Help,' the chief repeated. 'Help us with our supernatural problem. Is that it?' I tried to crane my neck around to see him. There were three others in the room besides the two young men holding me in place.

'Do we cuff him?' asked the man to my right, his breath warm on my neck from his proximity.

'No,' said a woman, another cop by the look of her but one in plain clothes, another detective perhaps. I thought I had seen her before somewhere. Maybe this morning at the station.

'Yes,' countermanded the chief, frowning at his subordinate.

I let them do it. Stopping them would do me no favours, but as they turned me around, I got to see the chief and woman properly. They were standing next to a third man, a studious looking gentleman in his fifties who I recognised as one of the coroners.

'Oh,' he said, recognising me in turn.

The woman was average height and slight of build with curly brunette hair and dark brown eyes. To me she looked like a stereotypical mother in her late thirties. He wore a dark grey trouser suit and shoes with a low, blocky heel. Her blouse was unbuttoned at the top to show a silver necklace, but other than a wedding band, I saw no other jewellery and there was very little makeup employed. All in all, I judged that she dressed for her age and wasn't trying to catch anyone's eye. I *had* seen her this morning. I recognised the streak of grey in her hair. Then I spotted a massive incongruity: she was carrying a Louis Vuitton handbag. It was a limited edition one that cost a small fortune, and I recognised it because Kerstin had bought herself one last year. She made a big thing about it at the time, stroking it like it was a pet. I was intrigued enough to look up what it was and gasped when I saw the price tag. What was a police officer doing with one?

'David Beckermann's mark is the same as the other victims?' I asked.

'Yes,' said the woman. This time the chief held up his hand to silence her, a rude gesture but one I thought she was used to by the lack of reaction she gave him.

The chief pierced me with a glare. 'Why don't you tell me what the mark is?'

I gave him a wry smile. 'I only had time to look at it briefly for the first time last night when I found him. I have no idea what it is or what made it.'

'But you think it is something supernatural?'

'Oh, cut the crap,' I snapped, surprising everyone with my outburst. 'You have a pile of bodies and no idea what is going on. What I saw last night wasn't human.'

'I thought you didn't see anything,' Chief Muller replied calmly.

Knowing I had gone too far too fast, I quietened my voice as I tried to explain. 'Do you go to church?' I asked.

The chief tilted his head as he looked at me. 'Why do you ask, Herr Schneider?'

'It doesn't matter if you do or you don't, actually. The world is filled with religion. Lots of different ones, but most of them following the same concept of there being some kind of supreme being who created everything and there is a good place to go to when you are dead or a bad place instead depending on what you deserve. Lots of people believe in Jesus, right?' Next to me, one of the officers crossed himself, then saw the looks from his colleagues and became self-conscious, his face flushing. 'If you believe in Jesus, then you have to believe the whole thing, which means there are angels.' I paused for effect. 'And demons.'

The chief twitched his lips a little. 'You think the killer is a demon?' I got the sense that he was trying to keep the derision from his tone.

Looking right into his eyes, I said, 'I don't know what it is and I don't know if what I saw last night was the killer. It wasn't a man though.'

There was silence in the room. One beat. Two beats. Three. The chief continued to stare at me, trying to reach a decision it seemed. Finally, he spoke, 'I've met men like you before. Clever men: able to pick up on small pieces of conversation and use them to make it look like they are in the know. I don't know what con you are working, but I'm not falling for it. If I see you near this case again, I'll have you locked up and a psych team in to shrink your head so fast you won't know which way is up.' He nodded to the cops, who took my cuffs off. I rubbed my wrists and grimaced at the chief. 'Escort him out.'

The cop to my left moved a hand to place it on my shoulder. He intended to steer me to the door, but I twitched away from it, angry at being ignored and feeling impotent because there was nothing I could do about it. I wasn't going to back off, that was for sure. I was going to keep on this case until I caught the creature from last night and made him talk about the man from my kitchen. He had to know something.

The uniformed cops followed me until I was outside the building, the man on reception getting a stern talking to by the mortician as the doors closed. A huff of frustrated breath escaped my nose as I looked about for something to kick, but I brought myself under control and walked back to my car with forced calm.

As I drove away, disappointed with my efforts, I saw the female cop looking out of the morgue's reception window at me. She looked just as unfriendly as the rest.

A yawn split my face, reminding me that I needed sleep. I was going home to do some research and to get some lunch. Tonight, I would visit the hospital as I did every night, sad that I had been denied the chance to see Kerstin last night. Another yawn followed the first, and I made a promise to get a couple of hours shut-eye this afternoon.

I had no idea then that it would be days before I slept properly.

Chapter 4

At home, with a sandwich in my hand and a steaming cup of freshly brewed black coffee on the desk next to me, I fought my need to sleep as I searched to find what the internet might be able to tell me.

I was a regular visitor to the pages, sites, and groups dedicated to the reporting and cataloguing of supernatural or paranormal events, my own supernatural nature keeping me on the lookout for signs of others like me. Most of what they reported was absolute tosh, of course, but more and more over the last few years, I got the feeling there was some truth behind some of the reports.

This went back to the missing person thing I was talking about earlier. There were reports from people all over the world that their relative or friend or spouse or child had been taken. Some were just missing persons, but others claimed to have seen a person take them. I started reading the reports, my coffee going cold and forming a skin on it as I became absorbed in what I was reading. I tried to find key words, ones that would align with what I had seen, but that didn't work. On a pad, I made notes, writing down locations when I started to see a pattern. There were hubs of activity. Bremen and the surrounding area was one of them. There was another in Chippewa Falls, a small town in Wisconsin, America. Yet another in somewhere called Rochester in England. There were several others, including Berlin, and it didn't take me long to discern a localised pattern: where the people were going missing was grouped in hubs.

It wasn't just people being taken; there were stories of people seeing creatures that sounded remarkably like the one I fought last night. He had been disguised, my second sight revealing his true form, but from the descriptions I found online, some of them didn't bother to go to such lengths to hide themselves.

My eyes kept trying to close, so I went to the kitchen again for more coffee, making sure it was strong this time. Waiting for the machine, my heavy eyes drifted shut, snapping open again when my doorbell chimed. The unexpected sound in the quiet of my house almost made me wet myself.

The bell rang again, an insistent noise I had always hated but never found the time to alter. 'Hold on,' I said pointlessly as I walked to the door. A glance across the room to the wall and the clock there told me four hours had passed. It was the middle of the afternoon, and if I didn't get some sleep soon, I wasn't going to have time.

I could see a shadow moving outside through the frosted glass as I went down the three steps from my living area to my front door. I wasn't expecting anyone, which is to say that I expected the person outside to be selling something or conducting some pointless survey. I was surprised to find the female cop from the morgue on my doorstep.

I stared at her, a little dumbfounded and thus not saying anything.

'It's raining,' she pointed out, drawing my attention to the rain falling on her head. 'Can I come in?'

I blinked and shook my head to clear it, finally finding my manners. 'Yes, of course.' I stepped back out of her way and held the door, then closed it again to shut the cold outside.

'That's going to turn to snow soon,' she remarked, wiping her feet and looking about.

'I hope so,' I replied because it seemed like the thing to do. 'I would rather that than freezing rain.'

'God, yes,' she agreed.

Still standing in the little entrance lobby to my house, she puffed out her cheeks and looked at me. 'I'm Detective Lieutenant Heike Dressler. You're probably wondering why I am here.'

I decided to guess and make myself look scarily clever. 'You believe me about the supernatural thing and want to talk to me about it.' Her face took on a stunned look. I twitched my eyebrows at her and smiled in a bid to show her I was harmless. 'It was either that or my second guess.'

'Which is?' she asked.

'Actually, I don't have a second guess. Can I offer you some coffee?' I asked, leaving her by the door as I went into the house.

She followed me, looking around still as she walked slowly through my open plan living space. 'This is an impressive place,' she commented, her voice echoing through to the kitchen.

I didn't respond. I didn't want to get into a discussion about how I afforded it since it was all down to my wife, and she was not a subject I wanted to discuss with anyone. 'I take mine black,' I shouted back so she would hear me.

'Same,' I got in reply.

By the time I got back into my living space, she had taken off her coat and was sitting, looking comfortable yet poised, on one of my couches. I settled on the couch opposite her so we faced each other, a low coffee table separating us. 'I think you should go first,' I suggested.

She took the offered porcelain cup of coffee, sniffed it, and held it in her hands as she started talking, 'I am the lead investigator for this case,' she announced. 'That won't last for long. A special division from Berlin will be dispatched in the next day or so; the chief will not be able to resist them for much longer, not after the victims last night.' I stayed quiet as she paused to arrange her thoughts. 'We are under intense pressure and coming under a lot of scrutiny because we haven't managed to find so much as a fingerprint or a piece of fibre. The killer, whoever it is, is very knowledgeable. So knowledgeable, in fact, that it has caused speculation that it must be a cop or someone working in forensics.'

'I can assure you that is not the case.'

'You said you saw him last night. What did you see?' Her expression was hopeful. She wanted to hear that I genuinely knew something.

I pursed my lips, looking at her and trying to decide what I wanted to ask. 'Why are you here?' This was where I would find out what type of person I was dealing with. How honest would she be?

She flipped her eyebrows and smiled at herself, a lull in our conversation as she conducted a short internal debate. When she finally spoke, I got the truth, 'I am here because I am prepared to believe there are things in the world that we cannot explain.' She brought her eyes back up to meet mine. 'What did you see last night?'

There was something she wasn't saying, but her words hadn't been lies. I didn't answer her question. Not yet. I wanted more from her. 'That's not why you are here, though, is it? You didn't need to come to my house to make that statement. Tell me what you want from me.'

A flicker of annoyance played across her face. I wasn't giving her the answers she wanted. 'Look,' she said, 'there are bodies in the morgue, and I don't know why they are dead or who killed them. If you know something, I want to know what it is so I can catch the son of a bitch doing this.'

I relented, choosing a softer approach. 'I don't have a name for what I saw, nor have I encountered one before, but it was not human.' She didn't say anything, so I pressed on. 'It is man-shaped, but it wears an enchantment that disguises its features. When the cops turned up, it opened some kind of portal and stepped through it. That's why they couldn't find the person they saw me fighting when they came into the street.'

'They said it looked like a man,' she agreed. 'They gave a description, but they thought he was your intended victim. There's an artist's image being circulated already, and it looks human.' Her scepticism was to be expected, but she was presenting an argument rather than arguing with me. She wanted to know more.

I huffed out a breath; the next bit was going to be difficult. 'I need to know what you want from me. If it is just information, then I will tell you what I know. You will have to choose whether to believe it or not. If you want to involve me...'

'Involve you?'

'I have certain ... abilities. If you send cops up against this thing, it will kill them the same way it has killed all its victims so far.'

'My officers are armed,' she countered.

I looked right into her eyes. 'I'm not sure it will make any difference.' I didn't mean for my voice to sound like it was dripping with dread, but that's what she got anyway. I could see that it scared her for a moment, a flicker of fear appearing in her eyes before she quashed it.

What she said next surprised me. 'I saw something. When I was a little girl. I don't know how to categorise it. I was coming home with my parents late one evening, half-asleep in the back of their car when they stopped. We were in traffic, but there was something happening ahead of us on the road. There were men and women fighting, but they were using light that came from their hands, balls of light which they could throw. I couldn't see much, and it was dark, but the darkness just made the light display starker. I knew it was magic, real magic, not the silly illusions you see on television. Then they were gone. Suddenly, it was as if they had never been there. My parents denied seeing anything, pretending it was something I dreamed. But I didn't. Is that what you can do? Are you like them?'

It was a very direct question. I shook my head. 'I don't know what you saw, but I do know there are many things in this world that everyday people don't know about. Things that would shock their belief systems to the core. What you are up against is just one of them.' I was at the point where I had to show her something or push her away. Ultimately, I wanted to be involved in her investigation. There had been enough deaths; I was taking it personally now that I knew there was a supernatural creature behind it, but my desire to operate with the police ran deeper than that, my motivation to know more purely personal. Maybe the police could kill it. I wasn't confident though; I thought it more likely the creature would kill them if they ever trapped it. What that all meant was that I might be the only one who could stop it.

Heike was waiting for me, so I did something I had never knowingly done in front of another person, not even my wife; I picked up my wand and conjured magic into my right hand. Her eyes widened as I drew ley line energy through my body to form a glowing spark. Then I let my spell go with a word of command, and every open door in the house slammed shut. It was nothing more than a derivation of an air spell. Manipulating air was the first thing I learned, and I could control it confidently now.

The suddenness of it made her jump, a small squeal escaping her lips as she put a hand to her chest from the shock. She was staring at me and heaving in deep breaths as she recovered.

Holding her eyes with mine, I did my best to explain, 'I can control the elements - air, water, fire, earth. I draw energy from the Earth which allows me to create wind or flame and I can manipulate the elements to generate lightning. I can agitate the particles inside anything to create heat, and I can cause the temperature inside something to drop to freezing point. I have a few other skills, but if you want to ask me how I can do this, the answer is that I have no idea.'

'Are you a ... wizard?' she asked cautiously.

I shrugged. 'I'm something. There are a number of names: mage, warlock, wizard, sorcerer. They are just made up words from stories though. I don't know how to define myself, so I guess I might as well say I'm a wizard. My grandfather was able to do similar things, but with less power, I think. I saw him perform parlour tricks when I was young, but he died before my own abilities manifested.'

'Your grandfather?'

'Yes. He did magic tricks when I was little. I think that's true of a lot of grandfathers, but he wasn't pulling coins from behind my ear, he was making whirlpools in a glass of water and making objects move by pointing a finger at them.'

'So it runs in your family?'

I had to shrug. I didn't know if my grandfather got it from his father or grandfather or if he was the first. 'I get my looks from my grandfather, that was what everyone said. My hair is dark where my father's was light and receded where his did not. He was a little short for a man, and most would consider me tall. He was a little dumpy. He wore glasses, yet my vision is perfect. I had the same blue-green eyes of my grandfather, though no one else in the family had them. I think I got the magic from him so it would be fair to say it runs in my family but whether it went back any further than him, I couldn't say. I tried to ask my father about it a few times. Posing my questions in such a way that he would know I knew the truth and could talk to me about it, but he never got the hint. After a while, I concluded that he wasn't keeping his magical ability secret from me; it had skipped a generation. Neither of my parents had anything remotely magical about them. They were okay to live with; they seemed to take everything in their stride, so when my desire to cast spells resulted in a sudden quest for more privacy and a need to vanish into the countryside on my bicycle for hours at a time each weekend, it received little comment. I lost interest in girls and rock bands and even schoolwork for a while as I spent hours trying to work out what I could do.'

'Are your parents still around?' Heike was asking pertinent questions and it felt conversational, but I couldn't shake the feeling that she was using an interview technique on me to draw out more information. Not that I minded talking about it. Truth be told, I have rarely been able to share my secret with anyone and talking felt cathartic.

'My father died last year, my mother the year before that. I have some cousins somewhere, but I haven't seen them since my childhood. I don't have to write many cards at Christmas,' I joked. Then I fell silent for a moment, thinking about what I had just said. I describe myself as a wizard simply because it fits with books and films and stuff. There's no frame of reference, you see. I can do things that I cannot explain except by using terms like magic and wizard. Until I hit fourteen and my abilities manifested, I was just like everyone else and had no idea magic, the supernatural, or anything else out of the ordinary existed. Unfortunately, I was utterly alone. Sometimes I could see a glowing aura around other people; it told me they possessed some magical ability, or perhaps that they had the potential to wield magic, but I was yet to meet someone who actually could other than my grandfather. Actually, there was one exception to that statement, but I had given up looking for ways to ask people a long time ago. That was why I had been so surprised by the creature yesterday. It was only the second being, not counting myself and my grandfather, who I had ever seen who could perform magic.

My musings were interrupted my Heike. 'If we are not chasing a person, it changes a few things. The chief will have to ...'

'No.' I stopped her before she could get carried away. 'No one else is to know about me. If you tell anyone, I will deny this conversation and do my best to make you look nuts. I will help you,' I relented. 'I had to tell you this because the creature is able to disguise itself. It uses some kind of enchantment ...' I saw her looking at me in confusion. 'It uses magic that I cannot myself perform. If you were to look at it, you would just see the man your officers saw last night. One of my unique skills is the ability to see true forms.'

She was silent for a moment before asking, 'You were trying to catch it last night, weren't you? Why is that?'

Thankful that she wasn't able to tell if I was lying, that was exactly what I did, 'Someone has to stop it. I don't think anyone else can.'

Heike sat back, slumping onto the couch and tipping her head back to stare at the ceiling. 'I have approval to send officers out as bait tonight. We're dressing as homeless and will be spread all over the city, covering all the areas he has struck before.'

It might be a good strategy if the killer was human. 'That's going to get someone killed,' I assured her.

She brought her head back to level. 'If what you say is true, then, yes, very possibly. We must act. Doing nothing isn't an option, and I cannot tell him what you just told me.

He would laugh in my face, take me off the case, and the operation would go ahead with someone else running it.'

I nodded along. I felt sure she was right. 'I have more to show you.' I stood up as I said it, crossing the room as she hurried to follow me, and I started to show her what I found on the internet.

Outside, the winter sun was already beginning to dip, the light fading, and soon it would be dark. I hadn't managed a wink of sleep, and I knew for sure I was going wherever Heike was going tonight.

The creature was going to be out there, and it was time for round two.

Chapter 5

The rain petered out around half-past seven, but the steady drizzle made the street wet. It also brought the temperature back up above zero for the first time in days, not that being outside was any less unpleasant.

Detective Lieutenant Heike Dressler was one of the senior officers in Bremen. The task force of undercover officers on the streets tonight was her baby though she claimed to have argued against the concept. Under orders from Chief Muller, and unable to tell him the real reason why she didn't want to put the officers in harm's way, she sent them to positions most likely to result in a confrontation if the killer turned up.

It hadn't struck every night. There seemed to be little pattern to its appearances, but at this time of year, the officers, each of them volunteers as I understood it, would be hoping for a quick resolution to the case. That would be much better than spending night after night freezing their butts off on the streets waiting for an attack to happen.

Heike was in the Huckelreide district with two other officers. All her teams were set up like that so that no one was alone. I was with her, or rather, I was nearby. The other officers there didn't know about me, and she didn't introduce me. I just hid in the shadows and waited.

A whole lot of nothing was happening.

The officers all wore radios, the tactical kind that fit round your neck and pick up whispers so you don't give your position away by making noise. I couldn't hear them, but I had to assume there was communication back and forth between the groups.

Beneath a flyover bridge, the assembled homeless had a kind of shantytown going on. They knew who the officers were and had allowed them in because they knew about the recent deaths in their community. They were all warmer than me, heat from open fires and hot drinks being shared to keep the cold away. Set apart from the homeless group, I watched with some envy as Heike took a swig of something that had steam rising from it.

Because I was watching, I saw her react. Her hand shot out to grab the person next to her, and then three of them were on their feet. She was running in my direction, but not actually at me; she was going somewhere.

'What is it?' I shouted as I left my hiding place to race along with them.

'Two blocks over,' she shouted in reply, already starting to sound out of breath. 'Something is happening.'

'Who's this guy?' asked the man to her left. He was tall and hard looking, his crew-cut hair hidden beneath the hood of a sweater until his passage through the air pushed it off his head. He was giving me suspicious eyes.

'Special consultant,' Heike snapped back at him. Turning her attention to me again, she said, 'They said someone was approaching and then reported they were being attacked. Now nothing. Everyone is converging on their position, but we are closest.' Not if we had to run two blocks, we weren't. I was going for my car.

She'd thought of that though, the third officer, another young man, aimed his hand at a black BMW, the lights flashing as it unlocked, and we all piled in. The men in the front, Heike and me in the back.

Forty seconds of burning rubber, breakneck speed driving later, the man with the crew cut took a corner in a power slide and mashed the brake pedal to stop the car as we all saw the sight at the same time.

There were bodies lying in the street. Looking like crumpled rags of clothing, I knew each one contained a person.

'What the hell?' swore the driver as he produced a sidearm and exited the car. Heike and the third officer did the same before all three approached the first body. They were being cautious but also hurrying, scanning over their sights for any movement. There was none to see. Whatever happened here, we had missed it.

Seeing me approach them just as he bent to check the pulse on another person, the officer with the crew cut gave me a look that was meant to intimidate. 'He needs to stay in the car,' he snapped, the comment aimed at his boss, Heike.

She ignored him, as did I, dropping my second sight into place and looking around. Beneath the building to my left was a ley line, a big one. I could sense it without needing to look, but now that I was, I could see that someone was pulling on it. I had never seen this before. The snaking line of energy, which in my second sight looked like a fat golden thread beneath the earth, had a thinner thread coming off it which snaked up toward the surface. Was that what it looked like when I pulled on ley line energy to feed my magic? Following it up, I then saw the glowing aura of a supernatural creature. The image was distorted by the contents of the building, so all I really had was an impression of it, but there was undeniably something there.

I broke into a run. On the other side of this building was a magical practitioner, and I was willing to bet it was the creature I was looking for.

'Hey!' Heike yelled after me as I left her behind. There was no time for me to explain and I didn't want her, or anyone else, anywhere near this guy if that was who it was.

Someone was following me; I could hear their footsteps on the street as they chased me, though I didn't look around to see who it was. Instead, I began pulling on the ley line myself and reached into my sleeve to open the Velcro flap for my wand.

Caution as I got to the corner might have been prudent. I never gave it a thought. I ploughed on, rounding the edge of the building to come into the next street where I knew I was going to find my target.

I was right, but I was also wrong. Very wrong.

My second sight showed me the creature; it looked exactly the same as last night and even had on the same clothes. However, he wasn't alone; he had a gang of friends by his side, and I was crashing their party.

They all turned to face me, just as the hard-looking cop caught up to me. He had been chasing me, I think, but now he was presented with a group of what he thought were oddly-dressed young men. They were one street over from a crime scene, and he went into cop mode, pushing past me as he brought his weapon to bear on them.

With a word, I activated my defensive barrier, the shield invisible to all, but I knew it was there. Using my blood to invoke the spell tied it to me so that I could feel it even though I couldn't see it.

The officer growled, 'All of you, show me your hands right now.' He still looked like a homeless person but had a badge hanging on a lanyard around his neck. There was no trace of nervousness in his voice, he was utterly confident, continuing to advance on the gang as he called for backup. 'This is Officer Prochnow. I am in Niedersachs Strasse; assistance required. He touched his hand to the microphone on his neck as he spoke, ensuring a good contact with his skin so the message would go through clear. Now delivered, he placed the hand beneath his other hand to steady the weapon.

None of the creatures moved. He didn't see them as I did and possessed no concept of the danger he faced. He continued to advance toward them, his weapon trained on the middle of the group and ready should any of them show hostility or produce a weapon of their own.

Officer Prochnow inadvertently forced my hand. If I waited any longer, he would be too close; now was the time for me to attack them. Of course, no sooner had I thought that and lifted my hands in readiness to conjure than they attacked.

I counted twelve of them, and they moved as one. No word was spoken, making it seem as if this was rehearsed or they were able to communicate telepathically. They broke into a run, each of them pulling a black sword from behind their backs like the creature had last night.

Officer Prochnow dropped to one knee, making himself a smaller target but also getting into a more supported firing position.

As his first shot exploded from the barrel of his gun he shouted another instruction to them, this one equally ignored, but as I released my spell and pushed a jet of white-hot fire at them, I saw his bullet knocked from the air.

Officer Prochnow saw it too; I could tell from the string of expletives filling the air as he took another shot. His aim was true, but the creature he targeted whipped his sword down in an arc to strike the bullet. They would be on him in seconds, he was ten metres in front of me and exposed, Heike and the other officer yet to arrive, though I was sure they were on their way now.

The sound of sirens filled the night air, but they were way off still, and they wouldn't get here in time to help, not that I believed they could help regardless of when they arrived. My jet of fire was being deflected much as it had last night, the creatures using their swords to diffuse my spell, but as they bore down on me, I switched target, thrusting everything at the one creature Officer Prochnow was aiming at.

My jet of flame caught him by surprise, the tactic to distract him working perfectly as he used his sword to catch and deflect it but was then unable to stop the next bullet.

I'm not sure who was most surprised when it struck home. It caught the creature in his throat, snapping his head back and causing him to tumble into the creatures either side. They all looked stunned, each of them hitting the brakes and stopping to stare at their fallen comrade.

My jet of flame sputtered and went out as I lost my concentration, and Officer Prochnow lifted his head to see what damage was done.

Tumbling to the ground, the creature came to rest, bouncing once as his deadweight hit the street. After that, he didn't move at all.

'On the floor, all of you,' roared Officer Prochnow. His shout jolted me back to my senses. We could kill them; news which brought me joy. They were capable and strong, and they were able to fight my magic, but they could be hurt by human weapons.

Officer Prochnow drew in a sharp breath to shout again, but his command never made it past his lips. Before I could react, one of the creatures spun like a discus thrower and released his short sword. It hit Prochnow in his chest, tenting the clothing on his back as it went right through his ribcage.

I knew he was dead before he collapsed to the ground, and now it was just me with eleven of them. Facing off with twenty metres between us, I wasn't about to back down, and they would most likely kill me if I tried to escape. My only option was to fight.

Could I take on eleven at once? It was time to find out. The ley line was a strong one, tapping it filled me with energy even if not with confidence, so when I raised my wand and used it to push energy into the water molecules in the air, I knew I was going to shock them.

They didn't wait for me to complete my spell; they charged, again as one, but by then it was too late to stop me. The air around me felt warmer, the charge I built in it causing my hair to rise and I waited until the last moment, letting them come to me before I closed my left hand and released the bolt of lightning.

I had only done this a few times, always with unpredictable results and never against a living target. The blinding fork of light avoided me as I knew it would, spreading out from a point above my head to arc out like an explosion in every direction. What it touched, it damaged, picking up the creatures and tossing them away to crunch against buildings or bowl down the street. An errant finger of the blast hit the building to my left, blasting a hole in it with an explosion of bricks and mortar.

It didn't get them all, and it didn't do enough damage to keep them down, all but one getting back to their feet almost immediately. But it bought me a little time and some space, the nearest of them now more than ten metres from me. Unfortunately, they were close enough to throw their swords now, the short weapon clearly designed for such use as they threw them with deadly accuracy. Only my barrier saved me, but after it deflected two swords, it was about ready to fail, and I would have to reset it at home before it would be operational again.

UNTETHERED MAGIC

It felt like minutes had gone by since I came into the street, but in total it was probably barely even a minute, a fact hammered home by the arrival of Heike and the other male officer, both of whom must have come running the moment Prochnow called for assistance.

Coming into the street at a run with their weapons raised, Heike and the other officer saw Prochnow lying in the street. No longer liking the odds and shaken from my lightning blast, one of the creatures

raised its left arm to the rear and stepped backward to vanish through a pool of shimmering air.

All the others did the same, to leave the street suddenly empty and silent. Silent but for the wail of sirens still approaching.

Chapter 6

'What the hell just happened?'

The question came from the young officer with Heike. Both he and Heike still had their weapons trained on the point where the creatures had just been.

I didn't offer him an answer, I just slid my wand back into the pouch in my left sleeve and crossed to check the creature lying dead in the street. Using my second sight, I could see his ugly, reptilian face, but the enchantment was still working. Maybe it would fade, maybe it wouldn't, for now, though, everyone would continue to see man where I could see a creature.

Behind me, Heike and the young officer had rushed to check Prochnow. I walked over to them, where Heike was checking his pulse and looking unhappy. The sword had entered his chest just to the left of centre, penetrating all the way through to exit his back. It had most likely killed him instantly.

Heike locked eyes with me, neither of us saying anything though her young colleague was jabbering like a monkey, unable to process what he had just seen. She stood up again and placed a hand on his arm. 'Vogel, calm down.'

'They just vanished! You saw it too. They just vanished. They killed Prochnow and vanished.'

'Vogel,' she said, trying to get through his fog of confused panic. 'Vogel! Hans!' I thought she might slap him, but he brought himself under control.

'Sorry, Lieutenant. Sorry, I, ah ... sorry.'

'It's okay, Vogel. Just ... relax. We have work to do here now. Get on the radio and report officer down.' She could have done that herself, but he needed the distraction.

I moved, which brought her attention back to me. 'What did you find in the other street?'

'Bodies,' she replied bluntly. 'This is the worst one yet. Were they what you saw last night?'

I nodded in response. 'I'm going to check them.' I left Heike and Vogel with Prochnow and walked back to the previous street. I looked up at the sign: Droste Strasse. I had never been in this part of the city before; none of it was familiar, so checking the name of the road was just for reference. The sirens were getting close, though it sounded now like there were several groups or clusters of them all converging on our location from different directions. Which made sense because Heike had deployed manpower all over the city.

I didn't have much time before they would arrive, and I was certain they would push me out of the way the first chance they got. That was if the chief didn't just have me arrested. I moved quickly. There were four bodies here, which made it the worst attack yet. If it had always been one creature before, it made sense the body count would rise with a dozen of them here tonight. I knelt next to the first one, putting my right knee on the cold, wet stone of the old cobbled street for balance as I pulled back the fold of clothing to get a proper look.

It was a woman in her thirties, and she was a cop. Her badge was tucked inside her clothing on a lanyard like the others. Her weapon was still in its holster under her left arm. There was a mark on her neck. It looked like a love bite, or hickey. I used that parallel because what it really looked like was a suck wound, an exit point where she had been drained. Not drained of blood, the skin wasn't broken but drained of life as if the creatures were sucking the life energy out of their victims. It was the same as the one on David Beckermann, but now I was getting a proper look at it.

Her lifeless eyes stared at the sky, tiny spots of white visible in them as they reflected the tapestry of the stars above. I let her go and moved on to the next crumpled body. It was the same, though this one was an elderly man, his age somewhere around seventy and he was clearly homeless, his clothes ratty and dirty, not artfully made to look that way like Heike and the other officers.

I stood up as the sirens hit the end of the street. Three police cars swept around the corner and skidded to a stop as their anti-lock brakes caused the tyres to skip across the wet cobbles.

I made sure my hands were visible and empty, held out from my sides so there could be no confusion. When I saw DS Schenk's face getting out of the second car, I knew I would need Heike to stop him from arresting me no matter what I said.

I wasn't wrong. His very first words were to the two uniformed officers getting out of the car in front of his. 'Arrest him,' he commanded with a finger jabbed in my direction.

'Belay that order,' snapped Heike, entering the street once again. 'He is here as my consultant.'

Schenk scoffed, 'You got to be kidding me.'

She ignored him. Taking charge as the most senior officer present, she issued instructions to cordon off the scene, get the forensics team down, wake the chief and make sure he was on route if he wasn't already and get the fire brigade because apparently, my lightning blast started a fire when it blew a hole in the building in the next street.

I didn't get cuffed, but I wasn't allowed to play with the others. DS Schenk made enough noise that Heike relented and had me shoved out of the way at the end of the street. Being there meant I heard it when they realised someone was missing. They had five bodies if you included Prochnow, but as more cars arrived and Heike handed out yet more tasks, one of which was to round up as many of the homeless as they could find in the nearby streets, someone asked where Officer Nieswand was. They were missing a cop.

The officers present spread out, concern making them move fast as they searched for the missing colleague. Suddenly that was the most important task, and everyone was involved. They went searching for homeless people. It was clear there were more temporary homes than there were bodies, so some had escaped in the confusion of the attack, that was the obvious conclusion the police drew. Had Officer Nieswand gone with them? Had he run away? He was nowhere to be seen and wasn't answering his radio.

The worry between his fellow officers was palpable, most especially in Heike, who felt responsible. She was keeping a brave face on it, but I could tell she felt awful, guilt chewing her up inside for allowing the operation to go ahead when she believed what I had told her this afternoon. One officer had died in the initial attack, Prochnow was killed while fighting the gang of creatures, and now another officer was missing. It was a horrible mess.

Feeling cold and tired, and unable to take part in any of the activities, I found a police car that wasn't locked and climbed inside. I stretched out in the passenger seat and was asleep in seconds.

A hard thump on the window woke me after less than a minute. Schenk's face was staring down at me, an ugly disapproving sneer just before he yanked the door open. 'Get out.' I guess the car I found unlocked was his.

I didn't bother to argue with him. I just got out of the way so he could get in and went to find Heike. I soon wished I hadn't. She was off to one side, just her and the chief, and he was tearing into her.

'Two officers dead, another one missing, three dead civilians, a dead suspect, property damage? And you want me to believe you saw men vanish through a magic door?'

'I didn't say magic door,' she snapped, trying to keep her voice calm. 'There were men here, and they vanished, Vogel saw it too.'

'I'll explain what happened,' I growled before Muller could speak again. I approached from behind the man, so he hadn't seen me coming. I think he expected to find one of his officers when he turned to face me. Surprise quickly turned to anger.

'You! What are you doing here?' he demanded.

'I brought him along,' admitted Heike, her voice strong and lacking any sense of regret. 'I wanted to hear what he had to say. None of this is normal.'

'You're suspended, effectively immediately,' the chief barked in her face. 'Go back to the station and hand in your things. There'll be a formal review in due course.'

She stepped into his personal space, their chests almost touching as she sneered up into his face. 'This operation was your idea. I told you it was a bad one.'

He narrowed his eyes at her. 'The record will show you were leading it. It was your poor coordination and leadership that led to the deaths.'

'Frans,' she let her voice soften, pleading with him to listen, 'what about what Vogel and I saw? There were a dozen of them. Prochnow killed one, but it is a whole gang, and they vanished into thin air before our eyes.'

He shook his head slowly from side to side. 'All I see in the street is a dead cop. You need to rethink your statement before the hearing.'

My jaw dropped open in disbelief as I pushed myself in front of him. 'You're not going to listen, are you. No matter what anyone says, you're going to keep on letting these things kill people. You can't catch them if they don't need to obey the same set of rules. They are moving between this reality and another one using magic.'

'You listened to this idiot, Dressler? They move between realities and use magic? You don't need a suspension; you need a psychiatric assessment. Be gone before I submit the paperwork myself.'

Shouts from behind me brought their attention in my direction, causing me to about-face as well to see what was occurring.

'There's been another attack,' shouted DS Schenk, locking eyes with the chief just before he slid into his car and slammed the door.

The next second I was running, with Heike on my shoulder.

Chapter 7

My car got abandoned again, left behind at the stakeout spot near the flyover more than an hour ago when we raced to get to the first attack. Now I was in a car with Heike driving, and I would have to work out getting back for it later.

The latest report sounded like something different. More like a home invasion than the energy vampire attacks we had been dealing with. I had just given the creatures a name – energy vampire. It worked for now and was better than constantly referring to them as creatures. We were racing across town to deal with a different crime, but one no less macabre.

Suspended by her chief, Heike was ordered to leave the scene of the energy vampire attack and assured me that she was doing as instructed and going to the station to surrender her weapon and badge. She was just taking a winding route to get there.

It was in the car, while I had a little time to ponder, that a thought occurred to me. It was to do with the energy vampires. They hadn't drawn on the ley line at any point. They weren't weaving spells or conjuring magic by any means that I could see. They were able to open portals; it took magic to do that, and they wore an enchantment that changed their appearance. However, they did those things without drawing on the ley lines. Tonight, when I first caught sight of them in the next street, I had seen someone drawing on a ley line. If it wasn't one of them, it meant someone else had been here.

'I think there's someone else involved,' I blurted in the dark of the car.

She flicked her eyes from the road to look at my face. 'What do you mean?'

As she focused on the road again, I tried to explain, 'When we arrived in Droste Strasse, I could feel a ley line running beneath the building to our right.'

'A ley line?'

I stopped and backed up a touch. 'Ley lines are lines that crisscross around the globe, like latitudinal and longitudinal lines, but they carry rivers of supernatural energy.'

'Right. Obviously.'

I carried on. 'I could feel it because that is where I draw my energy from to perform spells and harness the elements. I brought up my second sight to look at it and what I saw was a thread of the energy being drawn off by another practitioner.'

Her head snapped around to look at me again. 'Someone else like you?'

'Maybe... I'm not sure. Someone able to draw on the ley line energy for sure. But when I got into the street, all I found was the energy vampires.' Her lips moved in the dark as she repeated my words. 'Sorry,' I backed up again to explain myself, 'that's what I decided to call them. I needed a name. I think they are sucking out the victim's life energy, life force, whatever you want to call it. I think that is what the wound on the victims' necks is and why the coroner cannot determine the cause of death.'

'That actually makes sense,' Heike murmured as she ran the idea through her head.

'Where was I?' I asked myself, losing my train of thought from explaining things and from general fatigue.

'You were saying about the other practitioner.'

'Oh, yeah. So, I don't think it was any of the energy vampires. I have never seen them wield the energy or conjure spells, so it makes sense that it was someone or something else and I worry that it might be whatever is controlling the energy vamps.'

'Someone that is ... what? More powerful?' Heike asked, her voice adding to the sense of dread I felt.

'The vamps just don't give me the impression they can do this by themselves. Also, and I know you won't like this, but the missing officer...'

'Nieswand?'

'Yeah, Nieswand. The vamps haven't taken anyone before that I am aware of. So, if he is missing, and hasn't just wandered off, maybe he was taken by the mystery guest.'

Heike didn't like that idea, but she didn't argue. 'You mean like the missing persons stuff you showed me earlier?'

'There was a common theme among the reports, something that came up repeatedly,' I reminded her.

'The reports of someone seen at the house.'

'The descriptions were always different, though,' she argued.

'Yes, I think that's why no one has ever looked at it more closely. Missing person reports are regular. People go missing all the time. Lots of them are found. Lots of them are not, and I have more experience in this field than most.'

'So what are you saying?'

'Right what I said at the start: I think there's someone else involved. A different type of supernatural being. One that can draw on ley line energy and is taking people.'

'Taking them for what?'

I pursed my lips and shook my head, staring straight ahead out of the car's windscreen but focusing on nothing. 'I really wish I knew.'

'We're here,' she announced, turning the car into the driveway of a very nice detached house. We were in Schwachhausen, an expensive and old part of the city where many of the houses had been standing for hundreds of years, at least. This was no exception, the Bohemian look of it spiking an irrational twinge of envy for the people who lived here.

There were already three police cars parked on the sweeping drive, including Schenk's, which meant he was already inside somewhere. I figured he would do his best to make our visit difficult and he didn't disappoint me. He even tried to stop us from getting in.

'You're suspended, Dressler.' He was blocking the doorway with his girth, his oversized waist almost touching the frame on each side, his posture daring her to try to get in.

His refusal to acknowledge her superior rank didn't go unnoticed. 'Listen, Schenk, you tubby piece of crap. Do you really think I'm going to get busted? Do you think I won't be back and still your boss? Oh, hold on, isn't your buddy, the chief, just a year from retirement? What's going to happen then? Hmmm?' He didn't have an answer. 'Oh, sure, they might bring in someone new. They might even give the job to Schmidt for a while, but he's already half-dead from drinking too much. Push your luck, Schenk, and I will be there to remember.' Then, threat delivered, she shoved against his left shoulder and walked into the house.

Just to be a dick, I gave him a smile as I passed him, saying, 'I'm with her,' as I squeezed by.

With that problem effectively neutralised, we could get down to the business of finding out what had happened here. We found a distraught couple in their living room, a large open fire dominating one end of the space. A uniformed cop walked across the room to join Lieutenant Dressler as she led the way in.

'What's the scoop, Berkel?' she asked, addressing the officer by name.

'The mother heard her daughter scream, ran upstairs to her bedroom and found a man holding her.'

Heike asked, 'Where was the father?'

'Not home when it happened. He's…' Berkel checked his notes, 'Herr Weber is the CEO of a pharmaceutical firm. He was in Frankfurt today; his flight got in at eight-fifteen this evening, so he missed the whole thing and got off the flight to a phone call from his hysterical wife.'

'Ok, so what happened with the man? Did he leave a message? Is there a ransom?'

'No, nothing like that.'

I drifted away as Heike continued to quiz the young officer. No one was paying me any attention, and Schenk was outside smoking a cigarette, probably licking his wounds and vowing revenge, but with no one to stop me, I climbed the stairs.

The daughter's bedroom wasn't hard to find, the door was open, and there were two cops in there, talking and taking photographs. One spotted me, a man in his forties wearing a neat waistcoat with matching trousers in a dark blue. His shirt sleeves were rolled up and the collar of his white shirt was open, a tuft of dark hair poking out of from his chest.

'Are you with the family, sir?' he asked.

'Special consultant,' I replied. 'I'm here with Lieutenant Dressler.' My answer ticked a box it seemed as he went back to his business without another word.

I went to the girl's bedroom door and peered inside. It looked like the room of a teenage girl. There were pictures dotted about, the girl that appeared in all of them clearly the missing daughter. She was pretty, with long dark brown hair and freckles across her nose. I figured she was in her mid-teens, but her exact age had little bearing on the case.

To bring up my second sight, I closed my eyes and reopened them. Looking into the room now, I got nothing new. I wasn't sure what I expected. The man who had been here probably wasn't one of the energy vampires, so I wondered if maybe there would be some residual ... something still here. There wasn't.

I made my way back downstairs where I found Heike talking to the parents. 'He didn't hurt you when he took your daughter?' Her question was aimed at the wife, a woman who looked shrunk and shrivelled, curled into her husband as if his presence made her feel better. Frau Weber was also ridiculously attractive, her looks explaining those of her daughter. While she looked like a model, she was too much on the shorter side to be professional and was currently clung to the successful man she had married. He was several years older than her, perhaps a decade even and had a look about him that suggested he was used to being in charge and in control and getting his own way.

Frau Weber sniffed deeply and blew her nose. 'You're asking why I didn't try to stop him. Any normal mother would have ripped him apart or died trying, right?'

No one argued.

'I didn't get a chance. He was in her room, but he didn't try to leave. When I got there, he was holding her like she was a rag doll. She just dangled from his hand like she was dead,' she sobbed, struggled, and got started again. 'I screamed at him, but he just smiled, and that was when I noticed the wall behind him.'

My attention spiked.

'The air was moving,' she continued. 'It was like watching water in the air but what was behind it wasn't the wall in Katja's room. Right before my eyes, he stepped into it, yanked her after him and was gone.'

'Darling, you're remembering it wrong,' her husband insisted, not arguing with her and keeping his tone soothing, but, like everyone else, not believing what she said.

Getting everyone's attention, I spoke, 'No, she isn't.' The wife's face turned to look at me, so I spoke directly to her. 'Did he say anything to you?' She shook her head. 'What did he look like?'

What she said next chilled the blood in my veins. 'He had these piercing blue eyes. It was the thing I remember more clearly than anything else. Deep blue eyes.'

Unable to stop myself, I crossed the room to get to her, falling to my knees by her feet. She stared at me in shock. 'What else?' I demanded. 'What else do you remember?'

'Schneider?' Heike wasn't sure she liked the look of what I was doing.

'Please?' I begged.

'He wore black. A black silk shirt with the top three or four buttons undone and black trousers. He looked dressed to go to a party. He had dark hair cut short and he had several days of stubble.'

It had to be the same one. 'Was he muscular?' I asked, fearing that I might prompt a false memory, but unable to resist asking.

'Yes. Yes, he was. Do you know who he is?' Now she sounded hopeful that I somehow knew who had taken her daughter through the mystic portal of shimmering air and would be able to return her.

I rocked back on the soles of my shoes and stood up.

'Do you know who took our daughter?' demanded the man, his voice filled with desperation and frustration.

I shook my head. 'I don't know who he is.'

'But you just described him,' one of the cops challenged me.

'Yeah,' the father was getting agitated now. 'You know what he looks like, so you've seen him before.' It was an accusation.

'I have,' I admitted. 'He attacked my wife.'

The mother gasped and put a hand to her mouth. I was scaring her more now.

'Hey, where's he going?' asked the father, seeing me heading for the door to leave the room.

There were more calls for me to stop and come back, but I was overwhelmed suddenly. The man who hurt my Kerstin had been here tonight. Was he the mystery player in the street with the energy vampires? Had he been in my house so he could take Kerstin but ended up hurting her instead? I needed to think.

Heike's hand on my shoulder made me start, my heart beating a fast staccato in my chest. 'You want to tell me what that was about?' she asked.

'Nine months ago, I came home to find a man in my kitchen and my wife collapsed on the tile. She had a lump on her head and was unconscious. Her brain was bleeding and swelling. They got it under control, but she is still in a coma and may never come out of it. It was the same man. He vanished through a pool of shimmering air in my kitchen, and I saw what looked like a country house and garden in the split second before the portal closed. I don't know who he is or why he was in my house, but I need to find him and get some answers. Maybe that won't bring Kerstin back, but it's all I've got.'

Heike processed what I told her, didn't waste time on notions of sentiment for my loss, choosing instead to ask a question, 'Where do you think he has taken the girl?'

'To wherever they go when they go through the portal, but I don't think he is the same as the energy vampires. Whatever he is, it's something different.'

She nodded and blew out a sigh. 'Listen, I really can't delay getting back to the station to hand in my things much longer. If the chief beats me back there, it will cause trouble for me. The review panel will be a pain in the butt without disobeying orders as well.'

I shook my head. 'We have to go to the morgue.'

Chapter 8

'You think we need back up?' she asked. We were minutes out from the city morgue, my second visit in the same day, a new low for me.

'Back up would be great,' I agreed. 'However, unless you know someone who can do what I do only a lot better, then I think we are on our own. Bringing anyone else here will just put them in danger.'

The idea hit me when I was telling Heike about the man with the blue eyes. I explained that he was different from the energy vampires, and I realised that the one Prochnow killed just looked like a regular guy to everyone else. I was the only one who could see the true form beneath the disguise. The body would be taken to the morgue but when they cut it open, would they find a regular person's body and organs inside, or would they find something else.

I had Heike phone the morgue, the unanswered call telling me everything I needed to know.

We left the house in Schwachhausen in the squad car, her heavy right foot propelling us across the city with the siren and lights clearing the route. The chief called her personal phone twice during the trip, both calls getting rejected. She already knew what he wanted, but the text message he sent her made it very clear: she had an hour to get to the station and surrender her badge and weapon, or she would be history.

I convinced her to ignore it. There were bigger issues at stake.

'If we get there and their phone is broken, I'm going to have to kick your ass. You know that, right?' she muttered in the dark.

I figured the energy vamps, or whoever was controlling them, wouldn't risk the chance that the humans would dissect the body and be able to learn something from it. Why risk it? I was gambling that they would come back for it.

It took us thirteen minutes to get there, but all seemed quiet as we jogged the last few metres to the doors. From the outside, the morgue looked normal. Lights were on inside and nothing was on fire. However, the reception desk was empty; no sign of anyone inside though there were still cars in the car park.

'This is a twenty-four-hour operation,' Heike explained. 'It never shuts. Not even for Christmas.' Rapping on the glass was getting her nowhere, so it was my turn to step up.

'Let me,' I asked, flourishing my arms so she would know I was about to do something mystic.

'You can open locks?' she asked. 'I thought you said you could control elements. How does that help you to open a lock?'

'Actually, I would have to burst the lock. I can draw moisture from the air and make it gather in the lock and then cause the temperature to drop until the water freezes. That, in turn, would force the lock to burst.'

An incredulous look on her face, she asked, 'How long does that take?'

'Way too long.' I smashed the glass with a handy rock I found by the path. The safety glass fractured into thousands of tiny pieces which showered down inside. The alarm went off; a wailing noise accompanied by a flashing strobe high up on the front of the building.

We were in, though, two steps inside were all I needed to find the body of the receptionist. It was a different man to the one this morning. This one in his forties, his hair and beard shot through with grey. His neck bore the same suck mark as the other victims.

They were here. Or, rather, they had been here. Whether they were still here remained to be seen.

'You should wait here,' I suggested. 'Or better yet, wait in the car. If they come your way, hit the pedal and escape.'

In response, she pulled her gun from its holster, checked a round was loaded and pushed in front of me. 'I'm the cop here, remember?'

'I thought you were suspended,' I quipped back.

'Huh. More like fired at this rate.' I didn't know how likely that was, but there was no time for idle chatter. I had my wand out and a spell ready. My second sight was working to show me multiple targets approaching ahead of us.

'Be ready,' I whispered as I selected a spell to conjure. I really wanted to raise my defensive barrier, but it was burnt out from the fight earlier. 'They throw the swords they carry,' I added so she would watch for it.

I couldn't use lightning in such a small space; it would blow the wall off the building and probably fry both Heike and me in the process. Fire was tricky too; because it would set the morgue alight with us inside it. That left air, which might work, but in the end, when the first energy vampire appeared in the corridor ahead of me, I went with water. It was something I had never done before. Not on a live thing anyway. It was just too gruesome to contemplate. However, I needed something that would kick their butts and I was done being polite about it.

Heike gasped and stared open-mouthed. That was when I realised she was seeing them for the first time. They hadn't bothered with their usual enchantment, so she was getting the full ugly effect. We could discuss that later, right now, I needed to beat them.

As the energy vampire sneered and raised its weapon, I reached out with my spell, pushing it with my wand and using my left hand to control it. Line energy here was weak, but I had enough to control the liquid inside the energy vampire. They say the human body is fifty percent water. I figured the energy vampire couldn't be too much different from that. When I first conceived this idea, I tried it on a frozen supermarket chicken my wife brought home to roast the next day. The result was spectacular.

This was no different.

As I summoned control of the liquid in its body, the creature started to contort. Another of them rushed into the corridor, Heike shooting at it to keep it back. The sound was deafening in the close confines, and her bullets were deflected just as they had been before, but it slowed its approach, which gave me time to work. Another appeared, so now there were three of them, two stalking toward us and one at the front which I was controlling.

Just as the other two caught up to the first, I pulled the proverbial pin on my spell, unleashing all the energy outwards. The energy vampire burst like a watermelon dropped from a height. This was good and bad. Good because it scared the heck out of the other two and proved I could kill them myself. Also, the vamp didn't seem to have been able to resist or repel my magic this time like they did with fire. On the downside, Heike and I were covered in gloop.

So were the other two but they were less concerned about that and more terrified that they might be next. They ran, leaving Heike and me behind.

'That was disgusting, Otto.' Heike punched my left arm. 'Can you warn me if you ever plan to do that again.'

She had bits of vampire dripping from her hair and the whole of the front of her outfit looked like a bloodbath at an abattoir. I figured I must look about the same. Let's just say I was glad I had my mouth closed when I exploded him.

This wasn't done though, I ran along the corridor, pushing a wall of air ahead of me in case any of the energy vamps thought it might be a good idea to jump out on me with a short sword. The air barrier would knock them backwards before they could get to me, at least, that's what I thought it would do.

The whole corridor was filled with gloop, the tiled floor was slick with it, and I made a mental note to think about the consequences next time I wanted to blow something up. Heike stayed on my tail, moving with me, her gun raised as we advanced.

There were going to be more bodies; there were more morgue staff who we hadn't seen yet, but we had to be sure, and we had to be certain the danger the energy vampires presented was gone before we alerted anyone else. Bringing the police here now would just create more bodies.

Without warning, the air barrier I created hit something immoveable. I just stopped going forward as if I had walked into a wall. I pushed, against it but was unable to advance. It was as if someone was pushing back with an air spell of their own.

'What's happening?' asked Heike, her voice a whisper. 'Why'd you stop?'

I pushed, but I couldn't move my spell forward. I would have to drop it to advance though I didn't have to wonder why for long, because the person preventing my advance entered the corridor from the other end. There were no doors between us to the left or right, just a rectangular tube of floor, walls, and ceiling.

As our eyes locked, I almost lost control of my spell. My second sight was still in place so I could see the figure conjuring magic before me in its true form. And that was a problem.

'You're human,' I gasped.

Chapter 9

The man wore an elegantly tailored suit. He could have been a businessman on a break or a doctor doing his rounds. The jacket and waistcoat were not your usual off-the-peg fare; they were something else, something … special. The answer popped into my head; they were an old style. The jacket ended close to his knees with tails at the back, and the buttons on it looked to be made from silver. His trousers and waistcoat matched each other but not the jacket and there was a chain running into one waistcoat pocket which had to connect to a pocket watch. He looked like he had escaped from a steampunk event. His dark brown hair hung below his collar, a natural wave from a parting on the left side giving the effect of a full head of hair. He looked a bit like a model from an aftershave advert.

I noted that he didn't need a wand to control his magic, something he found amusing in me when he glanced at mine and smiled to himself.

'You should run,' he advised. His accent was thick, but also a little clumsy, like German wasn't his natural language but one he had learned.

Neither of us was relenting, each stopping the other from moving forward by the air pressure spells we both conjured.

'Why should I run?' I asked. I was nervous about what it meant that I had met another human who could do the same as me, but I wasn't about to back down. 'Why are you here? Who are you?'

With no warning that he was going to do anything at all, he dropped his spell with a suddenness that caused me to lurch forward. But then he did something I couldn't expect; he gripped my spell and yanked me off my feet. Somehow, he was able to latch on to my conjuring and rip the air I controlled from my hands.

I was flung forward, losing my footing amid the muck and gore on the tile, but caught by surprise I would have fallen anyway. I pitched forward on the floor and could do nothing but watch as he sent a fresh blast of air to send Heike tumbling back down the corridor.

I heard her gasp in surprise as she tried to protect herself, the air whooshing from her lungs as she bounced and rolled.

'Questions, questions, questions.' The man spoke, but he hadn't moved. His hands were held loose but ready at his sides giving the impression he considered me to be no threat at all. 'Why are *you* here? That is a more interesting question. You have some skill, in an amateurish way, I suppose. But you can be trained.'

'Who are you?' I asked again. I was on the floor with the man looking down at me. He was superior in every way at this point and had the advantage. I put my hands down so I could get up, watching to see what he would do.

He wagged a finger at me. 'I think you should stay on the floor for now. I prefer you that way.'

Behind me, Heike groaned. She was hurt and wasn't getting up yet so there was little chance she was going to shoot the guy and save me any time soon.

Movement to my front brought my attention back that way just as the energy vampires emerged. They filed into the corridor behind the new player, securing my belief that he was in charge as they filled in flanking positions on either side of him and just behind.

'This is the one?' the new player asked.

The energy vamp nearest him nodded. 'He is becoming a problem.'

I was still sitting on the floor in the corridor. My position reminded me of my early days in kindergarten when we would all form up in the hall and sit cross-legged on the wooden floor to listen to the head teacher and sing hymns. It was a weak position because there was no easy way to get to my feet from here. I was badly outnumbered, my partner was down, and I was fairly certain the man I faced had significantly superior skills when compared to mine.

He crouched, coming down so his eyes were almost in line with mine. 'The shilt would like to kill you now.'

'The shilt? That's what those things are called?' It was obvious from the way he said it that I finally had a real name for them.

'Goodness,' the man laughed. 'You really are stumbling around blind, aren't you?' He twitched his lips back and forth for a moment and puffed out his cheeks as he considered his next move. 'I'm feeling benevolent today, so I'll tell you what. Surrender and come with me now. Your skills, while meagre, may still make you of interest to one of the lesser demons; one who has the patience to train you yet not the status to take on a better developed familiar.'

'Or?' I asked taking note of every word he said because I was learning something each time he spoke.

He gave an apologetic expression. 'Or I can kill you right now. The shilts will finish the job for me, of course. They need feeding after all. I'm given to understand that what they do is quite painful for the victim, though.' He was explaining it in a tone I might use if I were giving directions to a lost motorist. My death or otherwise was of no consequence to him.

I was desperate to know more, but he used the words demon and familiar in the same sentence and I doubted I would enjoy any part of that experience. He was cocky. And arrogant. So certain that I stood no chance that he had inadvertently given me an opening.

He would see, or probably even sense, if I tried to conjure anything, which is why I punched him in the face instead.

He never saw it coming and his crouched position wasn't stable. Had he put a knee down, it would have given him a better platform but not enough to stop my swinging uppercut from toppling him backward when it struck. As it was, my right fist caught him under his smarmy chin and carried on upwards, snapping his head back violently. It was a pearl of a punch; all instinctual and one of those that gets logged in one's memory with a bunch of exclamation marks behind it.

I was still sitting on my backside in the gloop and there wasn't a chance in hell I could get to my feet before two shilt pounced on me, so I threw everything I had into a pulse of air. It wasn't to push them away, which it did, but that was a minor side effect; I used it to push me backwards. The slippery floor was perfect for me to use as a means of swift escape.

All the shilt chased, a roar of rage from the toppled wizard urging them onward as they pelted down the corridor. I had enough momentum to continue the slide, so I switched to fire; to hell with the building at this stage, I was just trying to survive. Heike had to be just behind me now, and though I was still sliding, I would need to get up soon. The jet of fire was keeping them at bay but nothing more and it was already causing the floor to smoulder as they deflected it away.

I had heard Heike moving about and groaning right before I delivered the punch, but now I needed to grab her and get her to safety with me. She was up on her feet looking a little shaky and her gun was in her hand again. Could they deflect the fire and the bullets at the same time? The corridor was sufficiently narrow that only two and a bit could fit abreast at a time. For once that gave me the advantage. I wanted to blow more of them up using water spells, but I could only focus that on one creature at a time and doing so would let the others get to me.

'Shoot!' I yelled, shocking her into action as I sent another blast of fire. I had to keep turning it on and off because they were catching and deflecting it each time. The combination of bullet and flame did the trick, Heike's shots finding their way through to halt their advance.

As the front two faltered, so the ones behind it questioned their desire to continue advancing. The wizard was back on his feet behind them, and he was furious. With a bellow of rage, he rose above the shilt so his head was almost touching the ceiling tiles above. His eyes were crazy, his lips drawn back in a grimace of hatred. I don't want to say that he was flying, but that was what it looked like; controlling the air to create a cushion beneath him was my guess, but as that flicked through my brain, his right hand thrust outward like a gun to shoot tendrils of lightning from each fingertip.

I don't know what difference a shield would have made, but since I didn't have one, it was a moot point. The blast lifted me off my feet and it felt like every cell in my body was on fire for a second.

I hit the floor with my back first, the wind rushing out of my lungs even as I jarred the back of my skull and brought the taste of blood to my mouth. Did I just knock a filling loose?

Lord, I hurt. There was no getting up from the lightning assault. Nothing worked. In fact, I had so little control over my body at that point I genuinely worried if I would wet myself.

Heike was still firing, though it sounded like a distant boom heard from underwater now, my ears ringing from a battering my body couldn't take. When a shadow stepped over me, I figured I was about to get eaten ... whatever you want to call it, by a shilt, but nothing happened. Or rather, nothing happened to me. I could hear voices shouting and the gunfire was suddenly more intense.

Getting an elbow beneath my side, I levered my aching head off the tile. There were more cops here, and they were fighting the shilt and the wizard. I was still in a direct line with him; he was at one end of the corridor and I was at the other, back in the reception area where his lightning blast threw me. We locked eyes for a split second, then a shilt opened a portal and they all went through it, dragging their wounded with them.

The sudden silence was startling. It was broken a heartbeat later by the sound of a fire extinguisher as two uniformed cops tackled the fire.

I put my head back on the tile and stared at the ceiling. I was bone-achingly tired; I needed to get clean because I had guts in my hair and on my clothes, and I hurt as if I had just tried to get amorous with a walrus. I wasn't thinking about any of those things though. I was thinking about the man I just met; another human who could wield magic. It was a major revelation. For the last twenty years, I'd thought I was the only one. Now I knew I wasn't, but it didn't come with the joy I expected to feel when I dreamt of this day. Instead, it came with dread.

'Who was that?' croaked Heike, her voice sounding parched and exhausted. She had scooted across the floor because she also didn't have the energy to get up and was now sitting next to me where I lay.

I blinked a couple of times. He hadn't given his name. It was one thing he didn't reveal. He said plenty of other things though, and I needed time and quiet to think about them. I rolled my head so I was looking at her. 'I believe,' I said once I had her attention, 'that we are in a lot more trouble than I thought.'

Chapter 10

The cops arrived in force. Once I was up, I could see just how many people there were at the morgue now. The carpark beyond the broken glass of the door was a sea of flashing lights in the dark, each of them competing with the other to see who could cause epilepsy first.

Paramedics arrived, offering both Heike and me a check-up, oxygen, and treatment for the minor cuts and abrasions we had.

We were lucky to have been rescued; Heike's status as a suspended cop who then failed to report back to the station enraged the chief who dispatched no less than four patrol cars when he saw her location from the tracker on the car she took. The cops who showed up were there to arrest her and bring her in, me too probably, arrived right at the end of our fight, saw monsters wearing human clothes, and waded in. Two of them got hurt, the same blasts of lightning from the mystery wizard's fingers taking them out too.

What we had now was a growing stack of credible witnesses who all saw weird unexplainable stuff happening and were not about to change their stories. Among them was Heike; discredit her testimony if you like, but what about Officer Vogel and the eight cops who first arrived at the morgue? Add their voices to Frau Weber's report of a man taking her daughter through a portal of shimmering air earlier this evening and Bremen had become ground zero for supernatural phenomenon.

The cops found the bodies of six more morgue staff. Even the cleaner, there to perform late-night sanitary work in the toilets and offices, was dead. The poor woman was probably working the job at night on top of another job during the day to make ends meet and most likely had a child or children at home.

It pissed me off.

The chief looked bewildered when he arrived. This was proving to all be too much for him. He had a missing cop, two dead cops, a dead criminal who had been shot by Prochnow who was now missing from the morgue (the shilts *had* come to collect the body). On top of that, he had chosen to suspend one of his highest-ranking officers, had at least one kidnapping to investigate and now he had nowhere to send the bodies because all the morgue staff were dead.

They weren't all dead, of course. The facility being one which operated twenty-four hours a day, meant there were several shifts of people. The lucky ones hadn't been working tonight.

All in all, I think the chief was relieved when the task force from Berlin turned up. I was sitting in one corner of reception, out of the way and no bother to anyone. I wanted to leave, but until someone offered me a lift, I couldn't go anywhere. Calling a taxi wouldn't work as they would take one look at me and drive off rather than allow me to ruin their upholstery.

Even though suspended, Heike had been dragged into proceedings, but like everyone else, she froze and turned to see what was happening when the man on the loudhailer started shouting.

'Everyone stop what you are doing. Put down what you are touching and leave the building in an orderly fashion.' I saw them arrive; I think anyone at the front of the morgue did because they rolled up in a purpose-built semi-trailer with three kitted-out Land Rovers in front and behind it like a military formation. Each vehicle had a row of four bright spotlights mounted above the cab. They served no purpose other than to blind everyone who tried to look their way and to make the procession more imposing.

The chief went outside to meet them, a thankful look on his face now that he could hand the problem over to someone else, but it was only seconds later when Herr Shouty Pants started on his loudhailer.

Of course, no one moved. The cops looked his way and paused, and a few on the inside of the morgue bent down or moved around so they could squint out into the dark to see who was making all the noise. None of them stopped what they were doing or put anything down though.

Not until he started speaking again, that is. 'This is Deputy Commissioner Karl Schmidt. This operation has been taken over by the Deutsche Kriminal Investigation Bureau. You are now trespassing on my crime scene. In thirty seconds, my men will begin arresting anyone still inside the city morgue.' Then, after a two-second pause, he began counting backwards from thirty.

There had to be half a dozen cops in the reception area with me right now. They all looked at each other in confusion or bewilderment, all of them trying to fathom just what was going on. Outside, I saw the chief reach for the loudhailer; his voice would be recognised and obeyed, but the new guy, Schmidt, slapped the arm away and continued counting.

The chief, having already surrendered all his power, now had to raise his hands to cup them around his mouth as he shouted. 'Everyone do as he says. Put down anything you are holding and leave the building.'

Slowly, as the deputy commissioner's count got down to fifteen, the cops started to drift outside. They didn't seem happy about it, but some of them shrugged as if accepting that they could go home now maybe.

I waited for Heike to appear and went out with her.

All the cops were being dismissed by the commander of the new task force. I couldn't imagine what special skills they had that might allow them to do better than the local officers. So far as I could see, this was above everyone's ability to deal with.

I was dismissed as well, but as Heike led me back to her car, I couldn't help but notice a pair of eyes tracking my movement. Standing just a metre or so from the deputy commissioner, dark eyes beneath a military buzz cut watched me, a quizzical expression on his face as if sizing me up.

I held his gaze for a few seconds, decided he was just trying to make himself feel tough and turned away. It wouldn't be long before I found out how wrong I had it.

Chapter 11

In the warmth of her car, I fell quickly asleep, again snagging only a few minutes sleep before waking to find we were at Bremen police station and I had to get out. It wasn't her car, after all; it was an unmarked police car. The night had been hectic, to say the least, and we were both still covered in gunk.

My car was back at the damned flyover where we first set the stakeout so many hours ago. Heike would take me to get it, but first she had to surrender her badge and weapon and file reports on the shots fired. There was no avoiding it, she assured me. I didn't want to go into the station, so she opened her own car, and between us, we used blankets in her boot to cover the seats so we wouldn't destroy them as the gloop in our clothes continued to seep out.

I was asleep again before she got inside.

By the time she returned, two hours later, I had a terrible crick in my neck, but I felt a little more human. She had been good enough to leave me the key so I could keep the car warm, but I hadn't turned the engine on. I just borrowed the blanket from her seat and wrapped myself up; it was more energy and environment conscious.

'I'm going to my house,' she announced. 'You probably want to get your car and get home, but it's only a couple of kilometres from here, and I have to get out of these clothes. You can shower there and borrow something from Franz; you're about my husband's size. Okay?'

She asked if it was okay right at the end after already announcing that she was going to do it. I narrowed my eyes at her to make her think I was going to argue. 'Will there be breakfast?' I asked, making myself sound deliberately mock-serious.

She laughed. 'Yes. There will be breakfast.'

And breakfast there was. She drove into a nice neighbourhood and onto the drive of a nice detached house. I didn't know what a detective lieutenant got paid, but it wasn't enough to afford this place. 'My husband's a dentist,' she told me as if sensing the question in my head. 'He'll be having fun doing breakfast and packed lunches for four kids before school.' She sounded happy at his suffering as if perhaps he usually shirked such tasks. I could only imagine I would think it a privilege because I hadn't been blessed with children yet.

She led me around the back because they had tile in the kitchen, and she wasn't letting either of us step on the carpet in her house. Five heads turned to see the mother come in, her husband, Franz, starting to cross the room to greet her and then changing his mind when he saw the state of her hair and clothes.

'Mummy, what are you covered in?' asked a little boy. He was sitting at a breakfast bar facing the back of the house as were all the children, four of them in a line with her husband scurrying back and forth with boxes containing four lunches and a jug of orange juice to keep their drinks topped up. On the side, his own cup of coffee looked to have gone cold and he had a jam splat mark on one sleeve, which he didn't seem to have noticed yet.

'Mummy had an accident.' She pointed to me. 'This is my friend, Otto,' she announced as I shut the cold outside and stood on the tile, not moving until she told me where to go.

'Hello, everyone,' I said, making myself sound friendly despite the bizarre appearance.

Her husband shot me a quick wave as he started to back out of the kitchen, saying, 'I'm glad you're here, darling. I've really got to dash. I have a meeting with the other directors this morning.'

With deliberately saccharin coated patience, Heike said, 'Sweetie, have you thought that plan through?'

She got a, 'Hmmm?' in reply from across the living space because he was already putting items into a work bag in his haste to get out the door.

She gave him a two count then yelled, 'Hey! Mister!' This time he looked up. It was very clear who wore the pants in their relationship, his breadwinning not playing part in the dynamic. As she threw her sodden, muck-stained jacket on the floor and kicked off her shoes, he had a worried look, like this wasn't the first time ever this had happened. She led him from the room with a crooked finger of insistence, their backs departing around a door frame to disappear.

Which left me alone with four children all staring at me. There could be no doubt they were all siblings and all from Heike Dressler. The girls were absolute spitting images of their mother; even the haircuts were similar. The boys too bore the facial resemblance.

'Are you a criminal?' asked the youngest, a little girl of about seven with her front teeth missing.

Her eldest brother, who couldn't have been any more than twelve himself, sighed at her foolishness. 'If he was a criminal, he would be in cuffs. You're a detective, aren't you?' he said it braggingly, slowing off his superior age and knowledge to the little girl, then looking crestfallen when I shook my head.

'No, I'm what you might call a special consultant.'

'He's a wizard, alright, kids?' snapped their mother, bustling back into the room without the father who had most likely caught a double barrel of frustration and rage after the immensely fun night she had endured. Getting suspended was just the cherry on the top, I imagined.

'A wizard?' the eldest girl repeated first, followed shortly by the eldest boy.

If they wanted more detail, they were not going to get it because Mother didn't have the time or patience for any questions, nonsense, or resistance. 'Everyone get ready for school. Teeth brushed, shoes on, the bus comes in five minutes. Get moving.' When no one moved in the following two seconds, a rather insistent, 'Now,' was added in a low growl.

Apparently, Mum wasn't to be messed with. Maybe this attitude was how she got to be a detective lieutenant in a male-dominated environment. The kids scattered, the sound of them fighting to get to the bathroom first and then fighting to get their shoes on first echoed back through to the kitchen.

Heike poured me a cup of coffee from the pot and one for herself. It was warm but not hot, the dark liquid doing wonders for me as it lit me up from the inside and chased away the scuzzy feeling in my mouth. The kids all came back for a kiss, each one given carefully because Mum was covered in crud and when the front door finally closed, Heike started stripping off.

I turned away so I wasn't watching and wondered if I should be somewhere else.

She saw me tense up. 'Well, come on wizard: strip.' When my eyes flared, she dropped her trousers to stand in a pair of crud-stained socks and hold-it-all-in knickers as she undid her shirt. 'You've seen a naked woman before, right? I am not taking these clothes anywhere.' She sighed as she threw the shirt on the floor. 'There's a shower room to the left just along from the front door. You'll find a robe you can wear hanging on the back of the door. I'll be upstairs. I'll bring you some clothes. Then we'll get some breakfast. I am starving.' She paused a moment to throw everything she had on into her washing machine and to fetch a black sack from under the sink. 'Put yours in here,' she said as I took it.

Then she was gone, unashamed about her woman's body in her underwear. Not that I thought she should be. She was right about the naked woman thing, of course, though it had been nine months now. Every public pool in the country had a costume-free policy and dual-gender changing rooms. Nudity was no big deal for Germans, or at least it shouldn't have been, but I found myself feeling self-conscious nevertheless because I had looked at her when I shouldn't have.

I pushed the foolishness from my mind and ditched my own clothes into the black sack; they were good for nothing but the trash now and went to find the shower room.

It felt good to be clean. I was still weary, but the hot water revived me more than I anticipated, and the shower had a massage setting, so I stayed longer than politeness and decorum should allow.

When I shut the water off and stepped out of the shower, I discovered a pile of her husband's clothing waiting for me. She left me a pair of grey hopsack trousers. They were new and a good fit, if a little short in the leg. I also got a choice of shirts, selecting a white cotton one because it would go with anything, and a black lambswool sweater. I didn't take the offered underwear but accepted the socks because who wants to be out in sub-zero temperatures wearing shoes but no socks. His shoes didn't fit, so I was going to have to put mine on again. They were still by the back door.

I found her in the kitchen, warming pretzels. It would never be my breakfast of choice, but the warm, salty carbs with coffee ticked a number of boxes. 'Sorry about the domestic stuff earlier,' she said around a mouthful of pretzel. 'Franz … he can forget that my job is a little more demanding than his. A tough day for him involves a child who doesn't want to have his teeth cleaned. So, let's get this breakfast done and I'll give you a lift back to your car.'

I finished chewing the pretzel I had in my mouth and took a swig of coffee. 'I can just grab a cab. There's no need for you to leave the house again.' I prised a piece of pretzel out of the back of my mouth where it had got stuck between my teeth. 'What will you do now?'

She frowned at me. 'What do you mean?'

'We have a demon … maybe a demon. I guess I don't really know, but the dickhead wizard guy that kicked my butt, he said the word demon, so I'm guessing…'

'You really think there are demons behind this?' she asked. I could hear that the concept terrified her. I wanted to reach out and touch her. Put a comforting hand on her arm, but we had already seen each other more or less naked in the last hour, so being tactile felt inappropriate.

I figured the best thing was to just brush over it. 'I'm going back to the Webers' place today. The … demon,' I locked eyes with her. 'I don't know what else to call it. The demon that took their daughter. He's the same person ... demon, whatever. He's the one that hurt my wife. If I ever want answers, I have to get them from him. And the wizard, whoever he is, he is human. That means I'm not the only one on the planet and boy do I have some questions for him. He seemed disinclined to answer questions, though and he is clearly the one controlling the shilt. That makes him responsible for the recent spree of deaths.'

'Shilt?' she echoed.

I thought about it. 'Ok, yeah, I suppose you were knocked on your ass for that part. The wizard said the things I called energy vampires are actually called shilt.' I pinched my nose as I tried to concentrate on what I needed to do. 'What they are called doesn't matter. What matters is that people are getting killed and we now know who is controlling them. Then we have a secondary problem with the demon kidnapping a girl which might not even be connected. I think it is, but I don't know how, which is why my next move is to go back to see the Webers. The wife saw it all; there has to be a thread I can follow, something she can tell me that will get me to the next step.'

'I can't go with you.' It was a simple statement, but it was very direct and contained no ambiguity. 'If they catch me interfering now, I am done.'

'I understand. But I have to go. My motivation is mostly personal, but I have to consider that if their daughter was taken by a demon, the police will not be able to get her back.'

'Demons though, Otto? You ignored my question a minute ago.' I should have known she would notice me doing that. 'Do you really think a demon took her? What the heck is a demon anyway, other than a creature from a story?'

'What is a wizard?' I countered. 'You call me a wizard because you don't know what else to call me. I can do things that defy explanation only because we don't know how to explain them. Maybe the wizard we met at the morgue can explain them. Maybe whatever took the Webers' daughter can. A demon is a thing from a fantasy book or a nightmare perhaps, but what if those books are based on reality?' I got a horrified look from Heike, and even my skin prickled and made me shiver at the thought. 'What we know is that they can wield magic and can move between realms or dimensions or wherever it is they go when they step through the shimmering air and disappear. That's where the girl will be. That might even be where Officer Nieswand is. I take it there was still no word from him.'

'No.' She shook her head.

I swigged the last of my coffee, pushed my stool back from the breakfast bar and stood up. As she looked at me expectantly, I pulled at my clothing. 'I'll have this back to you in a couple of days.'

'Don't bother. He hasn't worn those things in years. What do you want me to do with your things?'

'Burn them, throw them in the trash, whichever is easiest for you. I doubt they are salvageable. Have you got anything I can use to clean my shoes with?'

She reached along the counter to grab a packet of disinfectant wipes, throwing them for me to catch. I had never used or even bought a packet of these before and couldn't work out how to get it open. She laughed at my efforts before beckoning that I hand them back. There was a tag on one side I hadn't seen. I guess they were a handy thing to have around in a house filled with children. They did the trick on my shoes too.

'You're sure you don't want a lift anywhere?' she asked yet again as I grabbed the handle of the back door.

'I'll Uber it,' I replied with a smile. Thankfully my compass, wallet, and phone had avoided the gunk bath the rest of me got, safely tucked inside my pockets. Now they were in Franz's trouser pockets along with my wand and keys and a few other items, and just as safe if no more shilts or anything else turned up to get me anytime soon. I bade Heike a good day and, yawning, she told me she was going to bed, which reminded me how little sleep I had racked up in the last two days. A cab would have to take me all the way across town to get my car, so I could then double back to get to my house. I could go straight home, but the longer I left my car where it was, the more likely it was to get vandalised, so I did my best to stay awake in the cab, somehow finding the least talkative taxi driver in Germany and arriving at my car to discover I was already too late.

Chapter 12

The wheels of my car were missing. As were the wing mirrors, the bumpers and the engine.

'Is that your car?' asked the cab driver.

I swore in response. I wanted to get home to bed, magically have eight hours sleep in fifteen minutes and get to the Webers' place again. Now I had a new distraction.

Glumly, I paid the driver, got out and called the first breakdown company my internet search came up with. They promised to get to me in under two hours.

Perfect.

The temperature inside my car couldn't be much above two degrees, I decided when I got in. Worse still, unlike Heike's organised family vehicle, I didn't have things like blankets in the boot of mine. It was probably a demonstration of just how tired I really was that I fell asleep anyway. A rap on the glass next to my head woke me with a start.

Before I could get the door open, the man was shouting through the glass at me. 'I can't tow this!'

I wanted to ask if he was stupid. I knew I wasn't and had patiently explained to the person on the phone that the car had no wheels. It wasn't necessarily him I had spoken to though, so, giving him the benefit of the doubt, I said, 'Of course not. I expressly advised that the recovery vehicle would either need to bring a spare set of wheels or have a flat bed and a hoist.'

He rolled his eyes, swearing about the idiots at the yard as he stomped off to swear at them in person via the radio in his cab.

That task complete, he came back to me, turning up the collar on his oil-stained jacket against the breeze. 'I'll have to go back to the yard and come back out with a different rig. You don't need to stay. I can bring it to your house or…'

'The Audi dealership. The one on Stresemann Strasse.'

'Yeah, I know it.'

'They are expecting it.'

'Did this happen while you were in it?' he asked, eyeing me curiously, like I might have slept through it. Maybe he thought I had been on a bender and this was where I chose to stop because I couldn't drive home.

I shook my head. 'Long story,' I said rather than bother with any kind of explanation. 'I'm just going to call an Uber,' I told him as I lifted my phone to my ear; I didn't want to seem rude.

'I can give you a lift,' he offered. 'Depending on where you want to go. It's too cold to leave you here, and you will need to give me the keys anyway or stay here until I get back.'

I knew it would be an imposition to ask him to take me home, but I could get him to drop me at the Webers' perhaps; it wasn't all that far from where we were.

And that's what he did. His cab was gloriously warm, the heaters spewing air directly onto me to thaw my semi-frozen fingers, toes, and face.

By the time we arrived back in Schwachhausen, I was starting to think I might have to strip a layer off. I thanked him for the ride and for promising to get my car to the Audi place to get fixed and let him go. The insurance would cover the car repairs, which was a good thing because it wasn't going to be cheap to rebuild my nearly new car. Thankfully,

I suppose, I still had my wife's car in the garage at home and could use that until mine was returned. Car problems were just a distraction, an annoyance to get in my way when I wanted to focus on the case.

I was cold again by the time I walked the length of the Webers' driveway to ring their doorbell. Waiting outside for the door to be answered, I had my gloveless hands tucked under my armpits to keep them warm and was shuffling my feet because standing still made me feel colder yet.

When the door opened, it was a new person looking out at me. She looked to be in her fifties and had a grandmotherly look about her already. Her hair was greying with no attempt to colour it, and it was styled into a neat, but quite rounded, cut. She wore no make-up and her clothes, while neat and new, were very functional, no concern for style or modern fashion, unlike Frau Weber who had the look of a woman who was all about style and what was new in the shop window. I tried to move toward the warmth, but she blocked my path. 'I was here last night with the police,' I explained. 'Are you a relative?' I figured she had to be a sister to one of the Webers' or maybe a friend or even a neighbour.

It was the last of the three, she said, 'I'm Maria. I live next door. Why haven't you got a coat on? You'll catch your death out there today.'

'Long story,' I replied, giving her my short answer just as I had the recovery guy. 'Can I come in?' I prompted. 'Catching my death out here.'

When I smiled and shivered, she came to her senses. 'Yes. Goodness, sorry.' She closed the door behind me as I crossed the entrance lobby to put my hand above a radiator. 'Please wait here. Who can I say is calling?'

I gave her my name and waited where she asked me to as she vanished into the depths of the house. I continued trying to warm myself, closing my eyes and reopening them with my second sight in place. I didn't expect there to be anything to see but knew it couldn't hurt to scan around. Instantly, I saw something I hadn't noticed during my previous visit: a ley line ran beneath the street outside. Not that the presence of one so close necessarily meant anything. I filed the information away in case it had later relevance.

'What do you want this time?' demanded Herr Weber, just as surly now as last night. I hoped I would see Frau Weber on this visit; she was more receptive and the one who might be able to tell me something.

I met his unhappy face with a smile, extending my right hand warmly for him to shake. He took it, decorum dictating that he must even though he didn't look happy about it. 'Herr Weber, I am here to help.' I fished a card from my wallet. 'I specialise in finding missing persons.'

Frau Weber appeared behind her husband. 'Who is it, Karl?' she asked, coming into the hallway. She had obviously been crying; her face was puffy and red, but her hair and clothing were just as immaculate as last night. Make-up, which had given her a flawless complexion last night, was completely missing today, rejected because it would be washed away no doubt.

'Frau Weber, I didn't get the chance to introduce myself last night. My name is Otto Schneider, I'm a licensed detective, and I specialise in finding missing persons.'

'He's the charlatan DS Schenk warned us about, Krissie. He's here to con money from us.' Herr Weber was already trying to edge me back toward the door. 'The police are investigating. Your assistance is not required.'

'There's no charge,' I assured him. 'I want to help get your daughter back, and I don't think the police will be successful.'

'Why not?' Frau Weber asked, moving in close enough to look up into my eyes.

Seeing the sideways look Herr Weber was giving me, I decided to bend the truth a little. 'You are aware of the recent murders?' I made eye contact with each of them. 'There were several more last night, including a police officer. The Bremen police already have their hands full. I am not asking you for any money…'

'Then you must be doing this for another reason,' snapped Herr Weber. 'What is it? Notoriety? What will you gain if our daughter isn't found?'

His wife sucked in a tear-choked breath. 'Karl, don't say that.' She put a hand to her mouth as she fled the hallway, disappearing through an open door. Karl didn't seem to care.

I turned so that I was looking directly at Herr Weber and fixed him with a hard stare. There's a number of skills that came with the ability to use ley line energy, but there was nothing magical about my ability to hit people with a withering stare. I held the stare for a three count, saying nothing until he blinked. 'I believe I can find your daughter. If I can, I will return her to you, and I ask nothing in return.'

'Why even come here, then?' Herr Weber growled to prove he wasn't cowed by me. 'If you intend to find her free of charge, why not just go and find her?'

'I need an item of hers.'

'What for?'

'It's for tracking.'

'Like with a dog?'

'Sort of. Look, I just need one item.' I really didn't want to have to explain this any further because I would have to lie about the whole thing. Herr Weber didn't come across as the sort of man that would accept that I was going to use it for a spell.

Frau Weber returned, her eyes freshly red. 'What sort of thing do you need?' she asked.

'An item of clothing. It must be something she has worn.'

Now Herr Weber stepped right into my personal space, his chest all but touching mine. 'An item of clothing she has worn? Krissie, call the police. This pervert is going to jail.'

I could have pushed him away. I could have conjured a spell and scared the crap out of him if I chose to, and I won't claim I didn't feel tempted. I thought I would achieve more by ignoring him, though. 'Frau Weber, the man you saw in your daughter's bedroom last night: Did he say anything?'

'Hey!' growled Herr Weber, not happy that I was ignoring him.

I moved away, taking three paces down the corridor to get to his wife. 'Frau Weber, that man has your daughter. Anything you can tell me might help.'

She sniffed deeply and sighed, a shuddering outflow of air that shook her body. 'There was something.'

'Krissie, don't listen to this man's idiocy.'

We both ignored him. 'What was it?' I took her hands as I asked, making contact with her to make her feel safe. 'What did you hear?'

'It was when I was on my way to her room; before I got there. I thought I heard a man's voice, that was what drew me there, and I was about to get upset because she's not allowed boys in her bedroom. All I could hear was an indistinct bass rumble until I got to her door, then, just as I got there, I heard him say something like, "It's time for your training to begin." Frau Weber was looking at the carpet when she spoke, but I could hear the truth in her words. 'It was something like that, something about training. Then he saw me, and that was when he stepped back through the pool behind him.'

'Krissie, you have got to stop with the nonsense about the man vanishing!' Herr Weber was getting angry. He was right on my shoulder and quivering with rage that I had defied him. In his position, he probably didn't have people challenge him or argue with him very often. 'He left via the door. He must have.'

'I know what I saw!' she screamed at him, the veins on her head standing out. I thought it probably wasn't the first time this topic had been discussed in the last few hours. Turning back to me, she asked, 'What sort of item do you need?'

'Hmmm?'

'Clothing,' she prompted me. 'You said you needed an item of clothing.'

'Anything. A sweater perhaps. A sock, if she wears such things.' Herr Weber had stomped off when his wife shouted at him, which I thought was better than choosing to shout back as I had expected he would. Frau Weber ascended the stairs, returning a moment later with a stretchy top in her hands. 'I took this from her laundry hamper. Will it do?'

I nodded. 'That's perfect, thank you. I cannot promise anything. But I will do what I can.'

Frau Weber leaned to one side to look around me, then, satisfied her husband wasn't there, she lowered her voice. 'What did I see last night?' She looked right into my eyes. 'You know, don't you, Herr Schneider. It looked like a man, but it wasn't, was it?'

I pursed my lips and shook my head slowly, left and right. 'No, I don't think it was. That's why I cannot promise you a result.' She was crying again, and I couldn't decide if I should pull her to me for a hug or not. Not that I cared if her husband returned and found the two of us. I didn't want to hold her to me because I wasn't sure how I would feel with my arms wrapped around an attractive woman. I missed the comfort of my wife.

'My number is on the card,' I told her as I backed away. 'Please message me so I have your number. I will update you once I have something worthwhile to report.'

Then I was back outside in the bitter cold. A few flakes of snow were falling, and I still had no coat, hat, gloves or scarf. I dialled yet another Uber and made my way to the road, Katja's stretchy top in my left hand. I was going home to change into my own clothes, fetch my wife's car, since mine was most definitely unusable for now, and I was going to get some sleep. I felt pressure to begin, but I was already struggling to remember what Frau Weber had told me; fatigue was fogging my brain. I should have written it down. Yawning at the side of the road while I hugged myself and moved about to keep warm, the need dominating my thoughts was sleep. It had been eluding me for the last two nights. Tiny snippets of poor-quality slumber were all I had been able to manage. Had I known what was ahead, I would have booked myself into a hotel and gone straight to bed.

Chapter 13

Despite my fatigue, there was no way I was crawling into bed until I had used my tracking spell to get a direction for Katja Weber. I could have done it outside the Webers' house, but then I would have wanted to go find her immediately, and I wasn't dressed to be outside. That wasn't the only reason though. Honestly, I didn't think the compass was going to find her.

Finally, in the warmth and comfort of my house, I set the coffee machine and switched it on. Then I pushed all other tasks from mind as I focused on finding Katja. With my compass in my left hand, I positioned myself cross-legged on the carpet and conjured an air spell. Personal belongings, jewellery, trinkets, things that a person treasures, take on a sense of the person over time. They contain an echo, if you like, of the person and I can use that to find my way to them. Like most of my skills, I discovered it by accident one day in my late teens. The neighbours had lost their dog, a yippy annoying thing called Boris, that snapped its teeth at me any time I even went near it. They were upset, so my father offered to help look for it in the woods near the house, and my assistance was included in his offer.

Boris had got out when someone left the gate open, so his collar was still at the neighbour's house, the lady there carrying it around in her hand. We looked for more than an hour, calling the dog's name and whistling for it, looking for tracks in the dirt and listening for a bark.

I was unhappy about being included, my favourite show was on the television, and I missed the whole thing because I was pressed into looking for a dog that hated me. A short while after we got back to the house, I was outside killing time before supper when I spotted Boris's collar and lead hanging on the fence. The neighbours were out looking for it again; I could hear the echo of their voices from the woods.

I picked up the collar for no reason I could remember afterward, but felt an instant jolt of something, like a pulse connecting me to the dog itself. Sensing that I might be able to find him, I glanced around to make sure no one was watching me and conjured some air with an instruction to follow the dog. This was long before I discovered the use of a wand would help to focus and refine my magic, so all the air did was create eddies as it spun around looking for somewhere to go.

It was trying to do as I wanted but lacked form. What I needed was a way for it to point a direction. Quickly running inside, I found an old toy flag, the type you stick into the top of a sandcastle.

'Are you coming in for supper?' my mother called through as she heard me thunder by.

'Not yet, ma.'

Her voice drifted out to me as I ran across the back yard, 'Five more minutes, Otto.'

I wrapped the collar around the mast of the little flag and jammed it into the soil. Then commanded the wind to show me which way to go and watched as the flag fluttered like the needle on a compass. Every few metres, or when I found an intersection of paths, I stuck it in the ground and tried again.

The neighbours were searching in entirely the wrong direction. If my magical flag compass was to be believed, Boris had avoided the woods in favour of running along the back of the houses. I kept going, excitement beginning to brim as my device led me on until I reached the back of a house in the next street.

Holding the collar and lead and looking politely hopeful, I knocked on their front door. A little old man opened it. I didn't recognise him even though we lived in the same area, but he wore house slippers and trousers a least a size too big, held up with braces over a vest which had silver chest hair poking through it. His face was lined with red veins, and he had an awful toupee that was a dark brown and perfectly formed above his silver eyebrows. I didn't even need to speak because he saw the collar and knew what I was there for.

Over his shoulder, he shouted, 'Liesl, there's a boy here for his dog.' I heard his wife making upset noises, the sound of her voice echoing out into the hallway. 'You had better come in,' the man said as he backed away from the door.

Ten minutes later, I walked triumphantly home with Boris on his lead. Oddly, he didn't snap at me that day or any day since.

Almost two decades later, I have perfected and improved the technique, swapping out a child's flag for a compass I have doctored to get rid of the steel needle. The needle now is a piece of wood, but it spins about just the same and points the way to the lost person when I command it to.

It took me a few years to discover that clothing works better than jewellery or trinkets; something to do with cells from the body becoming lodged in the material as we continuously shed our skin was my guess. The detail didn't matter because it worked.

I conjured the spell and set it forth. The needle spun. It continued to spin. I knew what that meant, and it was what I had expected, but I stopped the spell and tried again, getting the same result three times in a row.

Katja had been taken by a demon or a wizard or something. The man with the blue eyes had dragged her through the portal so my compass couldn't find her because she wasn't on Earth.

Cancelling the spell, I unfolded my legs and puffed out my cheeks as I considered my next move. I needed to get to wherever they went when they stepped through the shimmering air. For a moment last night, I saw a lush garden with a house in the background right before the portal snapped shut. What did that mean? It meant that it wasn't some hellish landscape filled with unspeakable creatures on the other side, that was something. To me, it had looked like the houses near Lake Lucerne in Switzerland, a place I visited a few times as a boy. However it looked, I was confident it wasn't anywhere on Earth.

UNTETHERED MAGIC

A rumble from my stomach forced me from the floor as I went in search of coffee and food. I hadn't shopped in several days, but I had enough supplies to make a sandwich with some four-day-old bread. With an apple, it passed for lunch.

Now I needed to consider what I could do to prepare myself for the next encounter with the shilt and the wizard. The man with the blue eyes was out there somewhere too; if I tracked down Katja, somehow following her to the place beyond the portal, would I have to fight him? I thought it likely, so there was yet another opponent with an unknown level of skill to face.

The wizard had defeated me easily; he called my skills amateur. No. Meagre; he used the word meagre but said I might be of interest as a familiar to one of the lesser demons. Doing my best to calmly analyse what he had done; I could see that the skills he employed were fundamentally the same as mine. He wasn't necessarily stronger; he was just better with them. Much like a green belt taking on a black belt, the belt itself signified a level of skill which should guarantee victory.

In most cases, but not all.

In simple terms, he operated as if he had been given training and I had been forced to train myself. So, I could attack with fire and air and earth, I could freeze and manipulate water, and I could hit him with lightning. But he had shot lightning from his fingertips, taking just a fraction of a second to create the static electricity required where it took me five seconds of concentration to do the same thing. That might not sound like a lot, but five seconds is forever in the middle of a fight. Not only that, he had torn down my air spell and ripped it from my hands, so he had the ability to affect the spells I conjured. Having never met another person able to use magic before, my opportunities to learn such skills had been nil.

My skills needed to improve quickly, or I might not survive the next encounter. I didn't know it for certain, but I was fairly confident the portals could only be opened at night. At least, there were no reports of attacks during the day. That meant I had several hours before the sun would set, and I needed to fill them with practice. I wanted to sleep, but I couldn't put off going to rescue Katja, and therefore I couldn't put off trying to prepare for it.

There was one other thing I wanted to do, which required a trip into town. It could wait a while though; I was going to try to make lightning from my fingers.

I put Kerstin's car on the drive because it meant the double garage was then empty. It was a big enough space for me to throw a few spells around in and devoid of anything much I could destroy.

Even with a coat and my winter boots on, I was still cold, but I danced around on the spot to keep the blood flowing as I used my wand to create another air spell and thought about the mechanics of grabbing hold of it. It had no physical form; that was the bit which was making my head hurt. I gave up after a while and tried the lightning thing. My method for forming lightning was to agitate the moisture in the air around me. It took a few seconds to make enough static electricity to use, so how had he shot it from his fingertips? The answer was obvious: he stored the energy inside himself. I wanted to give it a go, but I wasn't sure how to do it so was going to have to try a few things and find out what worked.

Trust me when I tell you I learned to send the lightning outwards using myself as the start point after I blew myself across a field the first time I tried to make it. It hurt like hell. This was the first time I had done it differently since, and I was being a scaredy-cat about it.

The limp charge, because that was all I felt brave enough to experiment with, earthed through me anyway and kicked me across the garage's interior to hit a wall. Lying on the ground while I contemplated just going to sleep now that I was horizontal, I thought about how the lightning travelled through me and what I could do with it.

Gritting my teeth, I forced myself off the cold concrete and back onto my feet to try again. I used an even weaker charge this time but focused on a position in my head where I could store the energy.

I let the bolt go, sending it from my hand straight back into my body.

Sitting on my butt in the corner of the garage again, I accepted that this was going to take a while to perfect.

An hour later, I gave up and went to buy myself a sword.

Chapter 14

'Will that be all, sir?' The man behind the counter was clearly pleased with his sale. I couldn't guess how much his average takings were but today was likely to see a spike. His trade had to be mostly tourists; who else would wander into such a shop? Yet here I was, buying swords.

The shop sat right in the middle of Bremen's tourist hub. Bremen is a picturesque city, the centre of it filled with streets too narrow for a car to pass and incredible architecture that somehow survived the intense bombardment the city saw in the early forties. Tourists flocked to it now, large cruise ships bringing them down the Weser to dock within walking distance of the best parts. I guess that was how this particular shop endured.

I must have walked in front of it ten thousand times in my life but never once gone inside. The tall but thin window at the front displayed suits of armour and ancient weapons, but inside there were paintings and tapestries and all manner of other tourist rubbish. I wanted a sword, though, and I knew the proprietor sold them.

There were lots of them if you could believe it, stacked on walls and stuck, point down, into umbrella stands so one could draw them out like a young King Arthur. It took me a while to find the section that contained what I wanted. It was clear the shopkeeper had a lot of low-quality reproduction rubbish for sale. They looked genuine but would break in two when used in anger for the first time. They were priced cheaper than the real things, which were hundreds of years old and heavier than I expected. I was sure he did a great trade with the fakes for people that wanted a sword to hang on a wall. But I wanted a real one that wasn't too long because I planned to wear it down my back just like Wesley

Snipes in *Blade*. In the end, I picked three. All were much the same size and style, and each had a sheath they slotted neatly into. At the counter, on display under a glass top, I spotted daggers and knives. I really wanted a gun, but such things were not going to be easy to come by and certainly not at such short notice.

I paid with a credit card, waited while the shopkeeper boxed them for me, because one cannot walk through the streets holding a sword, and went back to my car. My next stop was a hardware store. I needed a sharpening stone because weapon-grade swords are all sold with dull edges.

By the time I got home again, the sky was darkening and the snow, which had been no more than a few lazy flakes, was now beginning to fall in earnest. Soon I would need to begin the search for the wizard and the shilt, and I had an idea for how I might achieve that. I still hadn't managed any meaningful sleep beyond the couple of hours I got in my partly dismantled car earlier but trying now would mean I was asleep if they came for me.

Functionally, I was fine, so I settled on the edge of a couch and began the process of turning the first sword into something that might cut when used.

At a little after four o'clock, my phone woke me. I had fallen asleep on the couch, the half-finished sword resting across my legs. I almost skewered myself when I snapped awake and sat bolt upright. The phone continued to drill a hole in my head with its insistent happy tune because I couldn't find it.

'Otto Schneider,' I snapped in greeting when I finally located it on the carpet beneath a rag I used for wiping the swords.

'Otto, this is Franz Dressler. Is Heike with you?' Franz blurted the words, seemingly getting them out as fast as he could. The sleepy fog I felt was ripped away instantly as panic in his voice caused the same in me.

Too gripped by the potential ramifications of his question, I didn't answer straight away. As adrenalin filled my stomach like a bowling ball and made me want to vomit, I said, 'I haven't seen her since this morning.'

'She's not here,' wailed Franz at the other end. I heard him swallow, a gulping noise in my ear. 'She's not here and the house is trashed.'

'Trashed?'

'It looks like there was a hurricane. Everything is everywhere. I couldn't do this much damage if I tried.'

'Have you called the police?'

Franz sobbed. 'Not yet.'

I was on my feet. 'Do it now, Franz. Do it now. I'm on my way.' I disconnected, throwing the phone into a pocket. I was already convinced the destruction in their house was caused by the wizard we met earlier. I'd made the mistake many years ago of trying out an air-based spell in my bedroom. My mother made me clean it all up and I never did it again. The chaos reported by Franz sounded the same.

Why he had gone for Heike was what bothered me. It bothered me because it felt like a leverage move. At the morgue, he demanded that I go with him and I refused, so he took the woman he saw me with. I didn't know if that was the case, but to me, it felt the most likely scenario.

I took the half-sharpened sword, made sure my wand was in its sheath in my left sleeve and ran for the door. My wife's car is kept in wonderful condition, but it is older than me and can be a little temperamental. She loved it though and under any other circumstances, I wouldn't drive it in the snow, or at all, for fear of scratching any part of it. The silver 1961 Ferrari series 1 250GTE was an elegant car and one of the few four-seater cars Ferrari ever made. She cherished it, which was why, as I raced to get to Heike's house, I raced ever so carefully. The engine had all the power a person might ask for, but the car was built when anti-lock brakes were on the same list as spaceships.

I slid twice on the slick roads before slowing my pace even further. By the time I arrived, the task force from this morning was already there.

I chose to glide the car to a stop well away from any other cars in case applying the brakes caused another skid. Two men were on route to intercept me before I could get out of the car.

'No civilians,' the first barked. 'You'll have to move along, sir.' He was armed, a stubby black assault rifle hanging from a sling over his shoulder.

I proceeded to get out of the car anyway. 'I'm a friend of the family,' I tried to explain.

'Sorry, sir. No civilians,' the man repeated his earlier statement.

A loud whistle got our attention. It was the deputy commissioner, the unit's leader. He was pointing to me and gesticulating that the two men abandon their plan to send me away: He wanted to talk to me.

I took two paces in his direction, pulling my coat tight around me against the cold, but that was as far as I got because a crackle of light drew my eyes into the empty road. It was far lighter out than it ought to be at this time of the day because the snow reflected the streetlight and the moon, amplifying their effect to make it seem almost like daylight. All the combined light meant it was very easy to see the wizard crossing the road as he made a beeline in my direction. He had half a dozen shilt with him, flanking him on either side like an entourage, but they fell back as he advanced, looking like they planned to take no further part.

He raised his hands to either side, sparks of light appearing in each of them as he sucked in ley line energy. 'No escape this time, little man.'

The task force men, all in tactical gear and looking confident, moved in to apprehend him. 'Stop right there,' someone shouted as a dozen weapons were made ready and aimed his way.

The wizard turned his palms to face Heike's house where the task force troops were taking up positions behind cars and trees. With a whoosh of air, he threw a blast that sent most of them tumbling. Only those able to find something solid to hide behind were left standing. The shockwave of air was strong enough to shunt cars back, and a few looked like they might even flip.

The shooting started immediately, a shout from the second in command directing fire at the wizard but he lifted one arm as if holding an invisible cloak and the bullets deflected off it, keeping him and the shilt safe. It operated much like my shield, but I had never been able to test to see if mine would keep out bullets and I had to question if, like everything else he did, his was just stronger and better than mine.

Seeing how ineffective the task force was, I knew I had to act now. It was that, or he was going to kill someone. The stupid half sharpened sword was in the car though, the presence of a tactical police task force sufficient to convince me I should leave such things out of sight. So that left me with my usual arsenal of tricks which were all the same as his tricks but less refined, less diverse, and far weaker. I felt like a nine-year-old going up against a grown man. David and Goliath analogies notwithstanding, I was probably about to get my butt kicked.

The wizard hadn't stopped walking, but his progress in my direction had slowed as he dealt with the task force officers. I sent a lance of flame in his direction when he wasn't looking. Hoping I would catch him out with my first salvo. I got to be disappointed when he deflected it with a lazy sweep of his left hand. Then, as if to demonstrate to me how ill-matched we were, he sent his own jet of flame to engulf two of the task force's cars. They didn't explode like you see in the movies, but they would do soon enough because they were convincingly on fire.

I wanted to try the lightning again. Though it had been a painful learning process, through trial and error, I had worked out how to spool some of the energy inside my body. I didn't think it was enough, but if I could get close to him maybe I could do something with it. Thinking about getting closer took me back to the one thing I had tried on him that had worked. The only time I had been successful against him was when I ditched the magic and punched him in the face. He hadn't been expecting it, and that was partly why I thought a sword might be a handy addition to my armoury.

I wasn't going to be able to get the sword, but that didn't mean I couldn't take him on physically. As I stepped into the street, his face swung around to face me, and he smiled. Could I fool him?

I started running, my feet slipping a little on the snow, but not enough to throw me off balance; the snow was fresh and therefore not yet compacted into an icy layer. I threw air at him using my wand to focus the spell and my left hand to control and shape it. He lifted a hand to form his own air spell, exactly as I hoped he would, so I felt the pressure as our spells met. The exchange of pressures, neither spell giving, almost made me bounce off, however, just as I had counted on, the moment his spell stopped me, he dropped it again and pulled my spell into him. I tried to watch what he did this time, hoping to gain a clue from his movements, but as he grinned jubilantly that he was so dominant and more capable than me, he also realised I was coming right for him with less than two meters separating us.

I genuinely thought I had him. I was about to smash into his ribcage with my right shoulder, bowling him over while at the same time delivering my stored lightning point-blank into his body. I got to him, but he was more ready than I expected. As we collided, he whipped around, converting my energy into a throw so he could toss me across the snow. My right hand made contact with his waistcoat at which point I released the lightning, but he either saw it coming or knew how to deal with it because it went straight through his body and into the earth without doing him any harm at all.

As I slid across the almost frictionless street, he shouted over the sound of gunfire, 'It would be less painful for you if you stopped this foolishness. The death curse will break soon. You could have position and power in the new society, or you could be yet another slave. My master will find a place for you if you let him. This is the last time I make this offer, Otto Schneider. When next we meet, I will kill you.' All the while he had been talking, the police were firing bullets at him, and he was keeping them at bay with one hand.

'Do you have Heike Dressler?' I yelled.

'Yes, but she is of no interest to my master. She possesses no skill. Come with me willingly, and I will do my best to ensure you are sold to someone who will not get bored and kill you.'

'I think I'll pass, thanks.'

He narrowed his eyes at me. 'Then I will simply take you.' He conjured a new air spell, lifting me from the snowy ground on which I lay. Just behind him, a shilt opened a portal, the now-familiar shimmering air his escape route and my probable doom. He planned to drag me through whether I agreed to go or not. I knew I needed to get to where he was going, but I had a better plan than going with him now. I would get there later and surprise him.

I hoped.

No part of my body was touching the ground as I floated on his cushion of air, and that meant I had no leverage to stop myself. I flung my own air spell in his direction to check my movement, but once again he tore it from me which only propelled me faster toward the shimmering portal. So, I closed my eyes and felt for the moisture. There was snow everywhere, but that wasn't what I wanted. On the roofs nearby there were icicles; long needles of ice just hanging from gutters and the edge of roofs. They weren't very long, but they were solid and there were a lot of them, the result of the temperature drop when the rain turned to ice.

I threw them all at him. Whether I caught him out or there just isn't a way to deflect that many tiny ice bullets, or that maybe he was already working too many spells, they got through, peppering him with tiny shards of sharp, rock-hard, ice. I got the shilt as well, most of them already working hard to deflect bullets as the wizard's shield didn't cover every angle.

As a piece of ice got through, I saw him falter, and so did the task force, renewing their barrage as he stumbled back, holding his forehead where blood was already visible. For a hopeful second, when I saw a puff of red where a bullet nicked his arm, I thought the task force's efforts might do the trick. His shield was only down for the briefest moment though, just long enough for one bullet to hit home. Then, as the shilt converged on him, getting involved for the first time, he stepped through the rippling air and vanished, the portal snapping shut behind him with a barely audible pop.

I was back on the snow, cold but fired up with adrenalin from the fight. That was twice he had tried to best me, and I had slipped away each time. He wanted to take me with him, that much was clear. It was also clear that he was offering some kind of preferential slavery, which sounded like an oxymoron to me.

I got up off the ground, sliding my wand back into its sheath in my sleeve as the task force advanced and I thought about what else he had said. He said Heike was of no interest, but I wasn't sure what that meant. I didn't think it was anything good. Running his words through my head again now, very little of what he said meant anything to me. There was something about a death curse ending and a new society that would follow, and he suggested that people with skill - I assumed he meant magic - were the only ones of interest.

Of interest to whom? The people through the portal? He was the one who used the word demon and introduced the concept of a familiar. I thought a familiar was like a pet. In the Grimm tales, there were witches with familiars.

'I need to debrief you, Herr Schneider.' The voice came from Deputy Commissioner Schmidt as he joined me in the snowy street. Now that he was closer to me, I got to see that he was perhaps a decade older than I had first believed; he was just ageing well. A few faint laughter lines and just a dash of salt and pepper in the short hair by his temples betrayed his age to be late forties or maybe just the other side of fifty. He was short too and had the soft, doughy look of a politician. Over near Heike's house, coordinating most of the task force's men, was the guy with the crew-cut hair. In contrast to his boss, he looked like he ought to be in charge.

I skipped all the preamble and nonsense. 'Who are you? What is this task force? You just took on someone with unexplainable powers, and none of your men seemed surprised by it.'

'That is why I need to debrief you, Herr Schneider. These are troubling times and I wish to offer you our ... assistance.' He was telling the truth, his offer to help genuine, but there was also something mixed in with the truth, like he knew how to make it sound genuine even when it wasn't. It was a worrying thought; I had always been able to rely on my ability to divide the lies from the honest words.

UNTETHERED MAGIC

I pressed him for more information. 'You came here from Berlin, have there been more attacks like this?'

'This really isn't the place for this conversation, Herr Schneider. I can tell you everything you need to know but only when you agree to work for us.' He was deadly serious this time, no sense of anything hidden in his words.

'Work for you? I don't even know who or what you are. He talked about demons. What do you know about that? And another thing,' I said, holding up my hand to ward him off as he tried to guide me out of the street. He didn't like me using the word demon in public perhaps. 'You know my name, but you haven't bothered to introduce yourself.' When he announced his name outside the morgue, there was too much noise and too many distractions for me to tell if he gave his real name.

'My name is unimportant, but since you asked, you can call me Herr Schmidt.'

'Herr Schmidt?' I scoffed, knowing for certain that he was lying about his name. 'The most common name in the phone book. Listen,' I poked a finger in his direction, 'I don't know who you are, but I'm not about to align myself with a clandestine organisation who clearly know a lot more than they are telling the public.'

'The public cannot know what we know, Herr Schneider.'

'Oh,' I said, getting into his face. 'And why is that? Afraid they might be able to protect themselves and then wouldn't need you?'

Herr Schmidt remained unflappably calm no matter what I said or did. 'We really cannot discuss this in public, Herr Schneider.'

'No, you want to keep it all a secret until I have signed up to your club and have my own secret decoder ring.'

Herr Schmidt sighed. 'Ok, do it.'

I frowned at him, not understanding the comment. 'Do what?'

Behind me, a voice said, 'Yes, sir,' and I turned my head around just in time to see the man behind me fire a taser.

As I twitched on the snow, the only thought I could focus on was how this wasn't going to help Heike or Katja.

Chapter 15

I awoke to find myself in a cell. It had solid-looking walls, floor, and ceiling, and a glass front through which I could see a blank brick wall painted white. I was on a bed with a cover over me and a thin mattress between me and the wooden slab that formed the bed. I sat up, doing so carefully in case I was wobbly, but finding that I felt fine. The taser's electrodes had hit the meaty part of my right thigh, the obvious aiming point since most of me was covered in clothing several layers thick. My footwear had been removed along with most of my clothing, leaving me in my trousers and shirt. I wasn't cold thankfully, but when I placed my right foot on the floor experimentally, the floor sure was.

I could feel a bruise on my thigh where the tiny electrodes had entered my skin to discharge their voltage. It was insignificant as a wound but bore significance beyond that because it meant Herr Schmidt and his entire operation were not what they said they were. I was supposed to be finding Katja Weber and now Heike Dressler. Instead, I was trapped in a cell.

'Hey,' I called to see if there was anyone listening. I waited and tried again. 'Hey.'

'Don't bother, man. They'll come when they want to.' The voice came from my left. I crossed to the front of the cell so I could push my face against the thick clear Perspex. Doing so revealed nothing of interest; all I could see was the wall stretching out in both directions.

'Hey, do you know where we are?' I called out, but I got no reply. 'Hey, man. Come on; I just got tasered in a street in Bremen. I woke up here. Can you tell me anything?'

There was a gap of a few seconds before the man finally answered. 'It doesn't matter where you are. You are guilty, and they are going to lock you up and throw away the key. You might as well come to terms with it.'

'Whoa! Guilty of what? I haven't done anything.'

The sound of the man chuckling echoed back through the cells. 'Then I expect they will be right along to let you out any moment now.'

I tried a different approach. 'My name's Otto. Otto Schneider. I'm a licenced detective in Bremen. How about you?'

Again, I got a long silence before he answered. 'It don't matter, man.' His voice was a rumbling bass, far deeper than average and like the wizard, he sounded as if German wasn't his first language.

'Where are you from?'

'That don't matter either.'

'What does matter?'

Again the long silence before he answered and a groaning noise as if he was turning over on his bed and couldn't get comfortable. 'What matters, the man asks?' He paused before answering. 'I made a mistake.'

'What did you do?'

This time I got nothing but silence, and no matter what tactic I tried, he wouldn't start speaking again. In the end, I gave up.

I had no sense of time. If I had to guess, I would say we were underground, but all my senses were shut off. I couldn't open my second sight; I couldn't tap into, or even feel, a ley line. I was defenceless and resourceless at the same time. All I could do was wait. Wait for them to come along when they were good and ready, just like the man said.

From the clock in my head, that happened about an hour later. The sound of a door opening and closing somewhere in the distance and then footsteps coming down the corridor in my direction alerted me. I got up from my prone position as whoever it was got within a few metres, hoping to see who it was even if they were not coming to my cell. I could hear the man in the next cell getting up too.

The footsteps kept coming, the face of the deputy commissioner appearing a few seconds before he reached the front of my cell. He walked within touching distance of the far wall, and I found out why as he came by the cell next door.

A heavy clang echoed as the man in there started screaming blue murder. It sounded like he was trying to smash his way out. 'Get over here, Schmidt, so I can unscrew your head! You had better pray I never get out of here.'

Schmidt paused to respond. 'You won't get out.' That was all he had to say, and he turned away as the man in the next cell started threatening him again.

I, too, was boiling with anger but trying to keep a lid on it. I couldn't do anything from my cell, so I needed to win him over and get out of the cell first. Then I could think about escaping.

'Herr Schneider, how long your stay here lasts will depend on how cooperative you are.' I listened for whether it was truth or lie, but that ability was shut off from me too. Angry at my predicament, I focused on what he was telling me. 'I need to know how you do the things you do. You will need to explain your abilities to my team of scientists, and you may be given a chance to work with us.'

So much for keeping a lid on it; I was instantly apoplectic with rage. I was so angry I couldn't speak, but the deputy commissioner filled in the blank space I left. 'Herr Schneider, I have much to discuss with you if you are prepared to listen. The world is not what you think it is, nor will it ever be again. I need your skills so that we may fight against what we believe is to come.'

I forced myself to calm down, sucking air in through my nose and blowing it out through my mouth. He was giving me one of the things I craved most: information. However, I had pressing questions of my own. 'What are you doing about Heike Dressler and Katja Weber?'

'What would you have us do, Herr Schneider? Do you know where they go when they step through their interdimensional gates?' It was a rhetorical question, my very favourite kind. His head was tilted to one side like a dog as he awaited my response. 'Neither do I,' he said even though I hadn't spoken. 'We suspect, as I am sure you do, that both ladies have indeed been transported to wherever they go, but we have no means to get there ourselves.' The deputy commissioner paced a little in front of the Perspex, silently walking along to the edge of my cell then turning and coming back. He looked down at his feet all the while. 'Shortly, Herr Schneider, I will have guards come to release you from this cell. You will then be given the opportunity to join us.'

'What if I say no?'

He stopped pacing so he could look right into my eyes. 'Nothing, Herr Schneider. I cannot compel you to do the right thing.'

'The right thing?' I snapped. 'You lock me up without reason, taking me by force and against my will and you expect me to believe that you are fighting for the right thing?'

'Episodes such as the one you have found yourself embroiled in have been occurring for hundreds of years. In the dark ages, they wrote of demons and foul creatures. The general population believes such things are old folk tales, yet you know as well as I do, that they are true. How true is something we have yet to determine because we do not know what they are, only that they are not human and can move between dimensions.' I listened patiently since he felt like explaining some more of what he knew. 'These episodes have been growing more common and are occurring in more and more places. Bremen is new. The first recorded incident here was less than four months ago.' I knew of one that occurred at an earlier date, but I kept quiet about it as he continued talking, 'One can track the acceleration mathematically. At the rate we are going, we will be in a constant state of attack in less than twenty years.'

Now I had to ask a question. 'Your little operation is set up purposefully to deal with it?'

'That is correct, Herr Schneider. We are a multi-national, borderless organisation, and we continue to spread as the political element of our operation makes contact with more nations. Fighting this in Germany will do us no good if the rest of the world falls.'

'Falls where? What is it that you think we are heading to?' Then something the wizard said came back to me. 'What do you know about a death curse?'

'A death curse?' he repeated my words. 'Where did you hear that?'

'The man I was fighting in Bremen. He said it to me when he thought I was beaten. He said, "The death curse will break soon." Then he went on to tell me I could be a slave or join with them and have position and power in the new world to come.'

'Are you sure you didn't mishear him? Adrenalin, the excitement of the fight can play all manner of tricks.' The deputy commissioner looked interested in me for the first time.

'I'm fairly sure,' I replied, running it through again in my head. I was certain I hadn't misheard what he said and couldn't come up with something else that might have sounded similar.

Suddenly the deputy commissioner was off, hurrying back along the corridor. 'When my team come for you, don't resist them. If you want to see daylight again, you need to cooperate.'

'Hey!' I yelled at his retreating back, pushing my face against the cool plastic again as I tried to see him. 'Hey! Let me out!' I got no further response from him, though. I wanted something to kick or throw, but there was nothing inside the cell I could pick up.

When the deputy commissioner was gone, the rumbling bass voice from my left said, 'He doesn't want you to join them. He wants to open your skull and find out what makes you tick.'

I didn't bother to reply. My mind was whirling with all I had learned in the last couple of days. So much of it felt like conjecture though. Were there demons? What exactly was a demon anyway? What was on the other side of the portal? With my head against the cool wall of the cell, I closed my eyes and laid out the problem into different components.

Then I looked at what I needed to achieve and what could wait. I couldn't save the planet, not in the next week anyway and I didn't know what I was trying to save it from.

I could save Heike and Katja, though. I could see a way to do that. Just about. It was going to take some luck and some skill and basically not caring whether I survived to get me through it, but if Kerstin was awake, it was what she would tell me to do.

There was one major barrier to my success that was currently quite unavoidable: I was stuck in this cell.

Chapter 16

'How long have you been in here?' I asked, not really expecting an answer.

To my surprise, his voice came back immediately. 'Eight days. If you're thinking about how you can get out of here, then you might as well stop wasting your effort. These cells are buried below ground and controlled electronically from somewhere else. There are no guards coming by to check on us ever. Our meals come through a panel at the back of the cell, which opens and closes electronically. If you try to hurt yourself, then and only then will the guards come, but you won't like it when they do because they will knock you out and restrain you until you promise not to do it again.'

'Do you have any powers ... any abilities?' I let the question hang in the air for a few seconds before I pushed on. 'I guess people would label me as a wizard.'

I heard him move; in my head, I pictured him going from lying down to sitting up. 'A wizard? Are you kidding right now?'

'Not even slightly. I met someone else like me yesterday; someone who could wield elemental powers – what most people would have to call magic. Until then, I had no idea there were other people like me. I mean, it makes sense that there would be, but having never met one, other than my grandfather ...'

'Well, I'm not a wizard,' he said bluntly.

I waited. Then I waited some more. He really wasn't going to share any more information with me. 'That's it?' I asked. 'We are in this together, man. I'm telling you everything and hoping we can work together, but you won't even tell me your name.'

I felt like I was starting to whine, but instead of shutting down again, he started speaking. 'You are telling me things, but how do I know that any of it is true? How do I know anything about you? If you are a wizard, why don't you magic your way out of here?'

He had asked a relevant question at least. 'Something is suppressing my magic.'

'Probably best to just get some sleep then.' That was all I got from him. He was surly, that was the dominant characteristic. He seemed angry at himself for his predicament, but I might be misreading it. Difficult to know anything when he wouldn't talk.

I could find no point in continuing to converse with the man, so I gave up and focused on the problem I faced. I couldn't feel a ley line, that was the crux of the issue. If I could draw in ley line energy, I could bust my way out of here, but it made sense that the task force would know to put me somewhere I couldn't tap into the magical energy I needed. They seemed to know more than I had been willing to credit them for. What could I do without a ley line? Or could I get to a ley line by pushing deeper?

I closed my eyes and pushed out with my senses. I got nothing in return. At least not to start with. There were no ley lines anywhere within reach. It was a very odd feeling, like floating in a way, and my magic felt untethered. However, in my concentrated effort to find what I needed, I found tiny particles of ley line energy floating in the air like dust. It wasn't the same thing by a long shot, and there wasn't much of it but maybe it was enough. I guess I had never noticed them before; I had always drawn directly from a line; they were plentiful and like drinking from a bucket, whereas in comparison, this was like licking condensation off a windowpane.

After five minutes of focused effort, intensely drawing energy from the air in my cell, I could just about produce a spark at my fingertips. It wasn't much. It really wasn't much, but I was filling with hope because there was an endless supply of the particles. It would take an age to get enough for me to do anything worthwhile, but it was becoming an eventuality rather than a mere possibility. With that knowledge, I started to think about how I could use them to exit the cage.

There appeared to be no weak points, but there had to be an electronic lock, and an electronic lock could be shorted. It wasn't charity that drove me to include the mystery man to my left; it was survival instinct. If they had two people to hunt or chase, they might go for him first. Or, with him beside me, we might stand more chance of getting out.

'I will shortly be opening my door. When that happens, I plan to get out of here. Can I assume that you would like to come with me?'

His rumbling bass came back after a second or so, 'Don't tease me, wizard.'

'I'll take that as a yes. If you feel inclined, once I escape this place, I have to rescue a girl and woman and could do with a hand.'

'Rescue?' He sounded interested for the first time.

'A woman and a girl were snatched last night. Katja Weber was taken from her house. She is fifteen years old. Heike Dressler is a mother of four and a detective lieutenant in the Bremen police.'

I heard his feet hit the floor. 'Okay, wizard. Tell me how you plan to get out of here.'

It was a simple plan, though it was another forty minutes before I finally felt I had enough juice to perform the spell. It was only then that I remembered my wand. I didn't have it. Like everything else, it had been confiscated after they tasered me. So now I had to do this old school style which was something I hadn't done since I made the wand more than a decade ago.

I licked my lips and raised both my hands, gritting my teeth because I didn't want to waste any of the juice I had.

'Hey, wizard, what's taking so long?' shouted my mysterious friend.

I ignored him as I focused on pulling moisture in from the air. It was a struggle though; the air had to be filtered as they pushed it down here, and it was dry. I looked around and found my solution in the corner of the room. A supply of water was just waiting in the toilet bowl.

I had never done it like this but half the things I had done in the last two days were invented or adapted so I focused and drew the water up, creating a whirlpool that I could draw into the air. Without my wand, I expected to struggle, but I found it easy. I started using the wand in my early twenties, finding that it gave me more ability to control my spells. Forced to work without it now, I discovered I could do more with the limited magical energy I had available. It was as if the wand had been limiting what I could do.

I pushed those thoughts from my mind so I could focus on the water. Like a thin tentacle, I controlled it across the air and into the locking mechanism at the edge of my door. As it ran in, I threw a new spell at it, chilling it until it was almost, but not quite, frozen. The barely liquid water filled with ice crystals would run out that much slower. It ought to create the short I wanted, but just for good measure, I used the last of the energy I held to agitate the air. I figured I didn't need a lightning bolt to fry the electrics, just enough amps to do some damage.

I overdid it.

The little flash of lightning I shot into the lock lit the door up from the inside like a neon light, arcing in every direction as it flash-fried not just the lock but everything in the cell block. We were plunged into instant and utterly total blackness for a second until emergency backup lights came on to provide dim light overhead.

'What the hell did you do?' the mystery man asked with a degree of awe in his voice.

Aiming at nonchalant coolness, I said, 'I opened the lock.' I hoped that was true because I hadn't tried my door yet and it suddenly occurred to me that the lock might have shorted closed.

Thankfully, that wasn't the case, and the door slid to the side when I pushed it. Stepping out of my cell and into the corridor, I saw the mystery man for the first time. The sight startled me. He was the biggest man I had ever seen. He had to be two metres and some tall, and he was broad like a bear. He was also younger than I expected, mid-twenties maybe.

His physique was extremely muscular, like a bodybuilder on steroids and lean so the veins stood out under his skin. His dark blond hair was buzz-cut short like mine on the sides but long on top where it was swept to the left. It gave him kind of a boy band look with his perfect white teeth, strong jawline and blue eyes.

'They'll be coming for us,' he said. He wasn't looking my way and he wasn't waiting around either; he was already heading along the corridor, breaking into a loping run as he picked up speed. As I ran after him, I was drawing in energy from the air again, trying to get enough juice to be able to do something when I needed to, but it was taking just as long now as it had before.

At the end of the corridor was the door I heard the deputy commissioner use. It was thirty metres in front of me and our only means of escape from the cell block. The mystery man had it open by the time I got there. It was dark on the other side of the door too; whatever I had done to the electrics had wiped out a bunch of circuits.

'Stay behind me, ok?' the giant rumbled.

I didn't argue; I figured they could shoot this guy a few times before he would even notice; I was more than happy to use him as a shield. I went to step through the door, but an immovable arm blocked my way. 'Wait,' he whispered.

Then I heard it, the sound of an elevator approaching. A bar of light swept down a tiny gap in the wall ten metres ahead of us and just as it stopped, the man started to run, breaking into a sprint so that when the doors opened two seconds later, he hit the three men getting out like a runaway train.

They were all armed: full tactical gear just like the other task force operatives I had seen. They looked mean and ready and above all, well-trained, but the elevator still had power, so they were coming out of the light and into the dark and their night vision was non-existent. They didn't see him until it was too late. His attack flattened them with a shoulder barge, knocking all three to the deck where he towered over them on one knee and punched each one unconscious before they could consider getting up.

Next, he stripped their weapons, yanking them roughly from their inert bodies, and stood up. I got a shock when he turned around to look at me. I only caught a glimpse of his face outside his cell before he set off, but I could see it clearly now, and it was changed. Light from the elevator, unable to close because someone's foot was stuck in it, illuminated his face. His jaw was distended and filled with a row of awful teeth. The upper mandible was the same and his cheekbones were pushed out as if making room for more teeth inside. Worse yet, his eyes were glowing deep red.

I took an involuntary step back, but before I could even take my next breath, his face began to reset itself to normal, his mouth softening as the teeth receded and the evil light behind his eyes dulled until they looked normal again. He looked at me and seemed unhappy as if ashamed I had seen it. 'That always happens when I get violent. I can't seem to stop it. Other times, it's controllable, but never when I have to fight.'

'Are you a … werewolf?' I asked tentatively. I was aware that we didn't have time for a discussion, but I couldn't resist asking the question.

He shrugged. 'Maybe. I don't know. I know I can change form from one thing to another.'

'Are there any more like you?'

'No.' Then, angry, he stomped into the elevator. Once inside, he punched the light in the ceiling which extinguished when it smashed, then he checked the gun he held, threw it to me when he was satisfied and checked the next one. I caught it, but the uncertainty in my fingers as I held it made him raise an eyebrow. 'You ever handled a gun?' he growled. I shook my head. 'Perfect.' He blew out a sigh and punched the button to take the elevator up. I was still standing outside as the doors began to close, their motion prompting me to jump through the gap.

I wasn't happy about the concept of shooting my way out. Yes, they had imprisoned me and threatened to keep me there for an indefinite period. I was not, however, a killer. I was very certain about that and wanted to keep it that way. Blowing the shilt up from the inside was the only example of taking a life I could come up with, and it really was me or him, a murderous creature that sucked the life out of people for food.

The elevator travelled upward, the counter on the wall next to me telling us we were all the way at the bottom and had fourteen floors to get to the top. Whether the top was the surface or not, I had no idea. About four floors up, my concerns over using the gun all washed away as a glorious feeling of ley line power flowed into my body.

I closed my eyes, and my second sight instantly dropped into place as I reopened them. I was coming up through the earth, rising toward the surface and there, above my head, was a ley line snaking away to the east. I could feel it, I could see it, and I could draw on it.

I sucked in energy hungrily, discarding the assault rifle so it thunked on the floor as I filled my hands with an air spell.

'What the hell, man?' asked my shapeshifting friend as he stepped a pace to his left to get away from me. I was fighting my face muscles, which wanted to grin. I felt more powerful than I had before. Somehow, the wand, which I had used to control my spells, had been limiting my ability to channel ley line power. Yes, I could focus better with it, but now I realised I could do more without it; shift more energy for sure and perhaps I wasn't trading the focus I had always used it for. Maybe this was maturity for you. Maybe it was something else, but I felt untethered suddenly and wanted to cast away to see what I could do.

'Ready?' the shifter asked in his bass rumble. I glanced at the lights just as the final one lit up and the elevator car slowed to a stop.

Staring at the doors, and poised for them to open, I said, 'Just don't shoot unless you have to. I think I've got this.'

'Yeah, right,' he said, and there was a click as he took off the safety.

The doors opened to reveal the electricity at this level was working just fine because all the lights were on and that allowed us to see a room filled with men in tactical gear all pointing their weapons our way. I think they expected us to surrender, but whatever it was they expected, they did not think I was going to send a blast of air so strong it picked them all up and threw them across the room. It was like watching a bomb blast, but I was the bomb. No one got a shot off, and I had lightning buzzing in my fingertips, ready to go. Creating it had taken less than a second, so fast I hadn't even realised I was doing it.

The room was silent but for the groans of the wounded. I felt powerful. I felt magnificent. When the elevator pinged, it made me jump.

'Sissy,' growled the shifter as he pushed by me to get out of the car. 'Come on; we need to keep moving before they regroup. Give them time, and they will find defensive positions to stop us leaving.'

Crossing the room behind him, I looked at the pile of barely moving bodies. He was ripping weapons away from them with his right hand, creating a pile of them in his left. 'I used non-lethal force,' I shouted so anyone conscious would hear. Most of them had tumbled ten metres or more, taking desks and computers with them to fetch up into a tangled lump at the opposite end of the room. 'Please don't make me use anything else.'

The shifter threw his pile of guns into a corner and went to a door. Raising an eyebrow in my direction, he asked, 'You think they would afford you the same courtesy?' It didn't matter that they might not. I was my own person and I didn't kill humans. I hoped I could go to my grave still making the same claim.

Behind us, the elevator started back down; someone had to have called it, which meant there might be more troops coming up behind us.

'Ready?' the shifter asked. 'Waiting isn't doing us any favours.'

'What's beyond the door?'

He gave me a how-the hell-should-I-know look. 'You're the wizard. You tell me.'

He had a point, but my second sight didn't show me anything. It meant we could reasonably expect there to be no supernatural creatures on the other side of the door, but beyond that, I couldn't tell him anything useful.

Across the room, a man tried to sit up. He winced, and I could see he was struggling with a broken leg. I couldn't do anything for him, but I needed to make sure he wasn't going to try to fight back. I also had a pertinent question to ask him.

'Where are we?' I asked, helping him to straighten himself into a more comfortable position. He grimaced at me like he wanted to kill me, but the shifter had already taken his gun. 'The sooner we leave here, the sooner medical help can get to you.' I wanted to point out that I hadn't asked for any of this, but the words would be pointless.

'Berlin,' he hissed between laboured breaths.

I was in Berlin. Well, that was just perfect. Now I was angry. What the hell was I doing four hours from Bremen?

'Hey, wizard. Can we go now?' Over by the door, the shifter was getting impatient. I made sure the conscious man didn't have any other weapons with which he might shoot me in the back, finding an item of interest which I held up, considered for a second and decided to keep. The shifter was already opening the door when I got to him. Cautiously poking his head around the frame, he got a salvo of bullets in response. As he quickly slammed the door shut again, I got a surly look from him. 'I think we gave them enough time to get into position.'

I readied a lightning spell. 'I can do something, but we'll have to open the door again. How many were there?'

This time I got snark in his response, 'I'm sorry,' he said sweetly. 'I forgot to count. Shall I have another look?'

'Yes, please,' I replied, showing I could do snarky just as well as anyone else. 'Would you like to borrow some fingers to help once you get past ten?'

His eyes went red even as I looked at them, but if he was going to hit me, he missed his chance as the elevator pinged to announce it had arrived on our floor.

I held my breath as the doors opened and kept an air spell ready to cast at whatever came out. Nervous noises from inside the elevator were followed by a gasp of shock as the occupants we couldn't see caught sight of the ruined room. The gasp was from a man, but I could hear a woman's voice whispering.

'Come out of the elevator. You will not be harmed.' When I got no response to my instruction, I tentatively edged my way back toward the open doors.

'Come on, wizard,' growled the shifter, ever impatient. 'We don't have time to play nice.'

Inside the elevator were three frightened-looking people in lab coats, two men and a woman who all raised their hands to show they were empty when they saw me. 'Come on out.' I made it sound like an order, and they complied.

'There's no need to kill us,' one of the men blurted. He looked like a scientist which is to say he met certain stereotypes: mostly bald, with wire-framed glasses and a body that hadn't seen the inside of a gym since he left school. The second man was tall and thin, about a metre ninety but as lean as a broom handle. They were both in their fifties, but the woman was older and carried a glamorous edge, her hair and makeup showing that she put effort into how she looked.

'I have no desire to hurt anyone,' I assured them which caused three pairs of eyes to flick to the mound of broken men across the room. They had me there, but now I was faced with a dilemma because I couldn't escape this room and couldn't leave them wandering around while I tried to figure a new way out.

From outside a voiced boomed, 'You've got sixty seconds to surrender or we blow the door.' The shifter growled an interesting response which somehow had more cuss words than non-cuss words.

I faced the scientists. 'Is there another way out?' I asked. The three of them each looked at the other two. 'Look, you show us a way out, you get to go home, and the door doesn't get blown off its hinges killing half the people inside.'

The shorter of the two men opened his mouth to speak, but that was when I saw what the label on his lab coat read. I grabbed him. 'What does animal containment mean? What are you working on?'

As I grabbed his shoulders, he squeaked in fright and began stuttering. 'It's, it's, it's.'

The woman spoke. 'We have been able to contain some of the creatures that have been preying on humans. They cannot stand sunlight, they die if we don't feed them live animals, and we have to keep them underground or they open a gateway and escape, but we need to understand them if we are to defeat them.'

Could this be my ticket?

'What do they look like? Do they look human?' All three scientists looked surprised at my questions, but none of them answered and I had no further time. 'What floor?' When none of them answered, I screamed the question at them, 'What floor?'

'Subbasement level two,' blurted the shorter man.

'Hey, werewolf. We have a way out. Let's move.' I was all about action suddenly. I had a working plan to get Katja and Heike back, and it relied upon me doing something I knew I couldn't do for myself. My dream ticket just landed in my lap.

Probably. I hoped.

As the elevator doors closed, I could hear the scientists hammering on the door and shouting to the troops outside so they wouldn't fill them full of bullets when they opened the door.

'Didn't we just leave the basement levels? Where are we going, wizard?'

I smiled in the dark of the metal car. 'Somewhere new.'

Chapter 17

Inside the steel car, I readied an air spell. It was my go-to because it was the most controllable and versatile. It also did the least damage when compared with fire, water, lightning, and earth. There was no telling who or what might be beyond the doors when they opened. The shifter sensed the same thing, the large assault rifle looking almost like a handgun in his giant fist.

He had to crouch slightly as the elevator slowed; he was too tall to see out otherwise. 'Are you going to give me a name?' I asked in the near darkness. 'It really would be easier than just shouting werewolf, you know.'

He sniffed loudly. 'I kind of like it. You're the wizard, I'm the werewolf. All we need now is a vampire to complete the crew.'

'And maybe a zombie,' I added.

'Why is it that all the supernatural creatures come from the butt end of the alphabet? Zombie, werewolf, wizard, warlock, witch, vampire.'

It was a fun question and his first attempt at conversation. There was no time to answer though, because the light illuminated our intended floor and the elevator pinged our arrival.

The doors swished open to reveal a corridor. This one had a laboratory feel to it, or rather, it reminded me of a hospital. The walls were wipe-clean plastic surfaces, and the floor had the linoleum tile that got rolled out as one complete piece. It went fifty centimetres up the walls.

There was no movement, and the lights were on the same emergency backup system we had left behind on the cellblock floor.

Close to me, the werewolf asked in a quiet voice, 'What are we doing here, wizard? Is there a way out?' He didn't sound nervous, more like impatient to get on with the escaping part.

I crept forward; my movement deliberate as I tried to make as little noise as possible. 'I am looking for someone.'

He twitched his head around to look at me. 'You know other people in here?'

'This isn't a person.'

'You need to stop with the cryptic shit, you know that?' His surly demeanour returned as if it had never left, but I ignored him as I reached a pair of doors and pushed my way inside.

Beyond the doors was a lab; somewhere I could visualise the three scientists hanging out. There were lots of computers and screens but most of the other equipment I couldn't hope to identify. Except for a centrifuge. I gave myself a little pat on the back for knowing what that was. The computer screen shone brightly in the dim light, which created dark shadows in all the corners and edges of the room. It was a large space; maybe twenty metres by thirty, which made it six hundred square metres of floor.

A noise caught our attention, both of us swinging our eyes automatically in that direction, and I swore at myself for not having my second sight already engaged. Then I remembered that it didn't work down here, and that was when I realised how little stored energy I was holding. Berating myself for coming in virtually defenceless, I missed the creature moving from its hiding place.

The noise was the age-old, clichéd throw-something-so-they-look-that-way trick, and it had worked on both of us. I saw the shilt mid-leap, an improvised weapon in his hand as he flew toward the werewolf's head. I released the meagre air spell I had been able to conjure, sending a pitiful shockwave of air but the werewolf didn't need my help. He grabbed the shilt by the throat with one meaty hand, the shilt stopping instantly as a demonstration of just how strong my new ally was.

I started to shout at him, but my words got lost as a second shilt tackled me. He must have circled around to get behind me, but whatever the case, he was on me now and trying to gouge my face. I couldn't get my arms up to defend myself so resorted to thrashing around to throw him off. He was trying to get to my neck, his intention, I felt sure, to latch on and suck out my life force.

He was stronger than me and able to pin me in place. Fighting him off was a tricky proposition as I needed to get him off me but also leave him unharmed. It was vital I didn't kill him so when he was suddenly lifted away from me, I knew I needed to act fast.

I yelled, 'No!' as I clambered to my feet. The first shilt was lying in two pieces on the laboratory floor. Not that I could see both pieces, I could just see the head where the werewolf had ripped it off and placed it neatly on top of a desk. Now he had the second shilt locked under his left arm while his right hand was tugging at the shilt's jaw; he was going to do the same thing to this one. 'We need him alive!' I yelled into his face as I pulled ineffectively at his right hand for him to let go.

'You want him alive?'

'Yes, man! This is what we came down here for. This is our way out.'

He still wasn't letting go, but he released some of the pressure, so the creature's neck no longer looked like it was about to tear. 'What even is it?' he asked, staring down his chest and squinting a little to see it better.

I blinked and looked at the werewolf. 'You can see its true form? It doesn't look human to you?'

'Human? It looks like something I left in the toilet bowl yesterday.'

I shook my head to clear it; the werewolf could see the shilt as it was. It was interesting, but it didn't get us anywhere. 'He can open a portal to his realm. That's where the two women were taken and that's where I have to go to get them back.'

The werewolf cocked an eyebrow. 'To their realm? That sounds like the dumbest idea I have heard in a long time. How do we get back? What will we find there, for that matter?'

'One problem at a time, wolfman. We have no way out of this facility. This guy is our way out. From there we can work out the next step.'

Eyeing me carefully, he said, 'You suck at planning.'

'Do you have a plan?'

'Yes. I complete the change and kill anyone that gets in my way.'

My eyes widened in response. I was fairly sure he was serious. 'Let's just put that one on the backburner for a moment, shall we?'

Slowly the werewolf changed his grip so that he held the shilt's collar in one hand. The shilt's feet didn't touch the floor. It was conscious still, though it was gasping for air now that it hung free and it was looking around, desperately trying to find an escape route. I stepped right in so my face was a few centimetres from its. 'My friend is going to put you down in a moment. If you try to run away, he will just pick you up again and hurt you. He will enjoy that. Nod if you understand.'

The creature nodded slowly, never taking his hate-filled eyes from mine.

'Can you open a portal back to your realm?' I got no response though his eyes were staring into mine as if trying to work something out. 'I am offering you the chance to escape. You can return to your realm. You just need to take the two of us with you.'

He smirked. It was an automatic reaction, not one considered and then faked. 'You want to cross to my world?' His voice was almost laughing.

'Hey,' said the werewolf, giving the shilt another shake as if the humour would fall out.

'Can you open a portal?'

This time it had a more serious look when it answered. 'Not here. I'm too far below ground. That's why they keep us down here.'

I swung my eyes to look at my tall friend. 'We go back to the elevator. All my power came back about four floors up, so we take him that far and see what happens.'

'Do we have a deal?' I asked the shilt. 'You take us through, and we let you go. You can go back to whatever terrible rampaging you plan to do on Earth, but you have to take me to a specific place.'

'Where?'

We had eaten up enough time on this venture, and I was sure the task force would organise themselves and come for us soon. In fact, I figured the only reason they hadn't followed us down already was they knew we were contained.

I huffed out a determined breath and started back toward the elevator. Over my shoulder, I answered the shilt's question, 'I'll tell you on the way.'

Chapter 18

That he might not have any idea where I wanted him to take me was a concern that only raised its head when he asked me where I wanted to go. It wasn't like I had an address.

He didn't know the wizard when I described him. 'There are a lot of humans. They all look and smell the same to me. What makes this one special?' he asked.

'When he goes through the portal, I see a lush green garden with a large country house. The house is white. A man with piercing blue eyes goes there too.'

'Daniel's house? You want me to take you to Daniel's house?' he sniggered. 'I can do that. He will be pleased.' The werewolf bashed the shilt against the side of the elevator car a few times to knock the smile off its face.

I tried a different approach. 'He travels with shilts and they open a portal for him. Why is that?'

'Humans cannot move between realms by themselves,' he grumbled, rubbing his skull where it had been used to dent the wall of the elevator car.

'What is your realm? Where are you coming from? Is it another world?' I got no response to my questions at first, just a knowing smile. When he did speak, he said, 'I'm sure you will find out all about that once you are trapped there. You'll make a nice pet for someone.'

I didn't let his words anger me, nothing to be gained by it. 'Why would anyone want a man as a pet?' I asked.

Glancing at the werewolf to see if he was going to bash him again, he murmured, 'Status. Demons like to show off. It is a demonstration of things to come.'

'What things to come?' There was no time for an answer though, as I felt the ley line energy flow back again. I drew it in hungrily once more as the elevator slowed its descent. We could hear the task force above us, their angry shouts echoing as they called down the shaft to see who was in the elevator. I thought it entirely possible they would start shooting soon. With a nod in his direction, I said, 'Do it. Take us through.'

The shilt flexed the fingers of his left hand, the portal emerging from his palm as he opened it to form a shimmering disc of vertical waves. Like a circular pond hanging vertically in the air behind him, the portal was attached to his hand still by a thin thread, and yet we were still standing in the elevator car. 'You have to be touching my skin to travel,' it grumbled.

The werewolf, still holding the back of the shilt's jacket, used his other hand to grab its skull. I had to wonder if he could just crush it if he chose to. I grabbed its wrist, and together we all stepped into the weird, shimmering pool of air. It opened as my face touched it, revealing a lush garden beyond. Then, I felt a sensation of otherness, of being in two places at once and of being somehow stretched.

Chapter 19

As we came through the portal, I pitched forward, falling through air because the shilt had tricked us and opened the way through three metres off the ground. Neither the werewolf nor I noticed until it was too late, the shilt shaking himself free of our grasp as we fell. He fell too but opened another portal immediately, so he fell through it to vanish again.

I thumped into the grass, the werewolf landing right next to me with an explosion of swear words. I stayed down on my belly, reaching out a hand to touch my partner's arm in the hope it might still him. I knew nothing about our new environment, but I was willing to believe there were hostile things here.

I reached out with my senses, feeling the familiar thrum of a ley line in the soil beneath me. I pulled more energy in, noticing instantly that it felt different. It was a nuance though; a minor difference, like taking the Pepsi challenge and wondering what the big deal was because they both taste about the same. I had energy, that was something. Now though, the real challenge began.

'Wizard, where are we?' To my left, the werewolf was looking dead ahead at the house while his fingers ran over the assault rifle and made sure it was ready to go.

'Daniel's house,' I replied.

'He a friend of yours?'

'Not exactly. We haven't been introduced, but I would like a word with him about a personal matter. I'm pretty sure he took the girl, Katja Weber. He has an accomplice here also, the wizard I told you about meeting. I don't understand their relationship, but the wizard referred to Daniel as his master and the wizard is human, though I don't think Daniel is.'

'Why not?'

'Hmmm?'

'Why don't you think this Daniel character is human?' I missed his question the first time he asked it because I was thinking about what I needed to do now that I was here. A tracking spell was the answer. 'Hello. Earth to the wizard.'

'Yes, sorry. He can open a portal for a start. I don't think the shilt was lying when he said humans cannot do it.'

'So, you got us here. Now what? Lying on this cold grass isn't going to fill me with chuckles if that is your long-term plan.'

He was right about the cold. It was warmer here than it had been in Bremen; probably three or four degrees centigrade, but I had socks on my feet and a single layer of clothing on the rest of me. We wouldn't freeze to death, but hypothermia was a real risk if we stayed outside.

I crawled on my belly like a soldier in the mud, getting closer to the werewolf. 'I need to make a tracking spell. That should be easy, but everything I want is still on Earth.'

'What do you need?'

I sighed. 'To start with, I need an item of Katja's clothing. I had that, but it is still in my car outside Heike's house, assuming the task force didn't take the car. That's the biggest problem to overcome. I then need something I can attach it to that will allow me to see a direction. We also need to get ourselves some clothing, maybe some weapons, and I would really like to find something I can change into an amulet for protection.'

I got the raised eyebrow again. 'That's quite the shopping list. How about a six-pack of beer and some Twizzlers while you're at it? Let's make it a party.'

My werewolf friend was annoying. It seemed to be a speciality or a default setting. 'We need to get to the house. I realise we can't tell to any degree of certainty from here, but I think it is empty.'

'How can you tell, oh mighty wizard?'

'Second sight. If there were supernatural beings inside, I would be able to see them. That's assuming everything here works the same as it does back home.'

'To the house then,' he said, getting up. I made to follow, but he placed a hand on my left shoulder to push himself off the ground and in so doing, shoved me back into the dirt. It was a juvenile move.

I planned to stick to the edge of the manicured lawn, keeping out of sight as much as possible but the werewolf strolled in a direct line toward the target. When I made, 'psst,' noises, I got the finger in response.

If anyone was watching, they would see a large, confident man walking through a garden with a large assault rifle and a furtive smaller man popping up and down between bushes. I probably looked like an idiot. I was also fairly certain if anyone saw the two of us approaching, they would tackle him first because he looked dangerous, which might give me the chance to slip away.

Nothing happened though, my belief that there was no one in the house proving accurate. At a door which appeared to lead into a living area with a television and couches, I stared in bewilderment through the window. I could be anywhere on Earth. If the television had been playing a soccer match, I would not have been any more surprised than I already was.

With his hand on the door handle, the werewolf asked, 'Are we going in?'

'Is it unlocked?' I asked in return, surprised that it might be.

He turned the handle and yanked, breaking the points where the lock anchored. 'It is now,' he growled as he went inside. Following him, I saw he had trailed dirt in on his feet, smudges of mud now ruining the immaculate carpet and I almost told him off until my brain caught up with itself and closed my mouth.

'Okay,' I said, 'I think we should search this place. Weapons, a compass, any sign that our quarry has been here. I'll start upstairs, yes?'

'Okay,' he nodded. 'I'll look for a throw rug that looks like a demon embroidered it, see if I can find a pitchfork stand by the front door; they must be a pain to keep tidy.'

Muttering under my breath about his continual need to make jokes, I rounded the end of the banister, and started up the stairs. I had no idea if I would find anything at all, but I didn't expect to find children's bedrooms. What the hell was this place? The shilt called it Daniel's house, and it was the one I saw behind the wizard as he escaped me, and the one Frau Weber described too.

At this point in time, I was content to believe Daniel was the person I knew as *the man with the blue eyes*. I was in the realm through the portal, but I felt like I was in an English country house. It was *Alice Through the Looking Glass*.

I scoured the upstairs of the house, moving from room to room as I looked for any sign that the women had been here. My first priority was to find something I could use for a tracking spell. I found nothing. I did find a wardrobe full of men's clothing though, so for the second time in what had to be less than twenty-four hours, I put on someone else's clothes. There was plenty to pick from, including a selection of skiwear, so I elected to be warm and layered up. Serendipitously, the shoes I found fit me perfectly, not that I took ski boots to match the rest of my outfit, I went with a pair of hiking boots. Hoping my colleague had enjoyed better luck in his search of the lower half of the house, I went to see what goodies he had amassed: some weapons at least, I was sure.

Back downstairs, I found the werewolf in the kitchen. He was eating a sandwich.

'What the hell, man?'

'You wanted me to check the downstairs of the house. I started by checking inside the refrigerator. I can report that I found nothing demonic. He does have some nice cheese, though.'

My stomach growled as I caught a whiff of his food. Cursing myself, I grabbed some bread and made a sandwich too. I didn't mess around buttering the slices or rooting around to see if there was anything I might prefer; there were pre-sliced pieces of cheese in a pack and sliced bread. I stuffed it into my hungry mouth and began chewing, snagging a coffee mug from the drainer to get water from the tap. That was when I saw it.

Heike's handbag.

It was sitting on the floor by a dining table at the far end of the kitchen. My mouthful of sandwich almost fell out.

The werewolf paused with his second sandwich halfway to his mouth. 'Are you alright, man? You look like you have seen a ghost and if ghosts do exist, I don't want to know, okay?'

I put my sandwich down on the counter, neither of us bothering with plates. I needed to check I wasn't deceiving myself, but I wasn't. Her purse was inside with her face on the driving license and her name on all the cards.

'That's not really your colour.' I couldn't tell if the werewolf was trying to get a rise out of me or just entertaining himself. I heard his words, but they were lost in the background as my mind whirled: I had my focus. All I needed now was something I could use as my compass.

'Have you found a compass?' I asked, spinning on the spot to look at him, the handbag gripped in both hands as if it might escape.

'I found bread and cheese,' he managed around a mouthful of both. 'This machine doesn't run on air.'

Accepting that I was going to have to do this by myself and reminding myself that I was lucky to have him with me and not be facing this alone, I set off to search for the things

I needed. I got as far at the hallway when I remembered the kids' bedrooms and the first time I had ever made a tracking spell. One of the beds had bunting above it that I could use as a flag. Anything would do, of course, but the bunting was the first thing I thought of. At the top of the stairs, I remembered the amulet I was supposed to have looked for on my first search. On my second sweep, I found a jewellery box next to a dressing table in what had to be the master bedroom.

In theory, anything would do. I had to perform a fairly complicated spell on it and imbue it with my own blood to connect it to myself. Then, provided I was wearing it, and it was linked to me, I could call forth the protective barrier I needed.

If a man lived here, there was no sign of any jewellery for him, but the woman had a cameo ring that was ideal for my purposes. If I could get it on, that is.

Which I couldn't.

Even on the little finger of my non-dominant left hand, the ring still wouldn't go over the second knuckle. It was all I had, though; her other rings were no better, so I took it and figured I could try to stretch it or something.

Just as I got to the upper landing again with my two items in hand, there was a clatter from downstairs. It sounded like two swords clanging against each other.

Chapter 20

I ran down the stairs, swore because my feet wouldn't move fast enough, and jumped from about halfway. I landed two-footed on the hallway carpet, lost my footing, toppled, went with it and rolled to get back to my feet. Then I came up into a sprint and instantly saw what it was that I heard.

The werewolf had a sword in each hand and was fighting himself.

'I found swords,' he said, not bothering to look at me as he parried another blow. 'They were above the fireplace.'

I wanted to slap my face into my palm in despair, but I had too much to do. 'Are they any good?' I asked as I ducked beneath his imaginary opponent.

He cried, 'Ha!' like a 1940's film version of Robin Hood, twirled the sword in his right hand around to rip the one in his left hand away. It sailed through the air to land point down in the carpet as he thrust a killing blow into the foe he faced, gouging a hole in the wall in his effort. 'Take that, you varlet.' Then he straightened up and swished the sword to bring it upright in line with his nose. 'What's a varlet?' he asked, dropping his Robin Hood act now that his enemy had been thwarted. 'It feels like the thing to say, yet I have no idea what one is.'

I felt like slapping the sword from his hand, but he looked like he was made from granite, so I let it go, electing instead to pick up the discarded sword to inspect it. 'These are fake crap,' I announced, feeling the weight of them, 'Chances are they will break if you try to use them in a fight.'

The werewolf continued to heft his. 'I think I'll take one anyway.'

I made my way to the kitchen, calling over my shoulder, 'I have some spell casting to do.' At the hob, I bit another chunk from my sandwich as I opened drawers and cupboards to find a small saucepan and a knife. Setting them on the counter, I placed the cameo ring in the pan in readiness, then switched the kettle on to deionise some water by boiling it. I could have conjured heat into the water, but why do so when I had a gas hob at my disposal.

'Whatcha' doing, wizard?' the werewolf asked, rummaging behind me in the fridge for more provisions.

'Sealing a protective spell into an amulet that I can wear.'

'Riiiight,' he drawled, opening a carton of milk and chugging it.

The boiled water went into the pan and I set a flame beneath it all. Then I closed my eyes and reopened them with my second sight. The amulet looked like nothing at this stage, but I would know if the spell had taken only by looking at it with my second sight.

Forming a water spell in my right hand and guiding it with my left, I connected myself to all the molecules of water in the pan as they boiled and bubbled. Holding it in that state with my mind, I picked up the knife, cut a small incision in the end of the pinky finger on my left hand and let blood drip into the water. I came across the idea for a protective barrier spell when watching an old vampire movie one night. I couldn't tell you exactly what triggered the idea, but I left Kerstin on the couch as I went in search of things I might use to try it out.

I felt the werewolf's gargantuan presence looming over me. 'Shall I explain?'

He pushed out his bottom lip as if weighing up whether he could find enough interest to listen to me, then said, 'Sure. I'm certain it will be very interesting.'

Despite the sarcasm dripping from his voice, I tried to teach him something. 'In principle, the conjuring is nothing more than a combination of air and lightning spells. The amulet is porous like all metals are, so my blood, carried by the water, finds its way inside the metal. Otherwise, I need to fill the pan with my blood. Heating it just makes the process more efficient. Getting my blood into it imbues it with my signature. Then to activate it, I use a word. The word isn't necessary, but words have power, and it helps me to focus on what I want the spell to do. When activated, it creates a half-sphere of invisible energy contained within super-electrified molecules of air.'

'What can you use it for?'

'Its original design was to repel a physical attack, the person running into me meeting with a solid wall of energy. However, I can also use it to hit people with. I discovered that a couple of years back when I tracked down a missing person and found them with their kidnapper.' I got an impressed look from him. 'Needless to say, it took me a few attempts to get it to work. The only problem is that it is generally only good for one use. With a standard human physical attack, I might get two or three uses out of it, but I used it to repel an attacking shilt recently, and it was burned out almost immediately.'

'Why don't you just make more and have one on each finger?' he asked.

Trying not to show off my superior intellect, I smiled as I said, 'Because the trigger word would activate them all at once.'

He frowned deeply. 'Can't you just use a different word for each one?'

As I opened my mouth to point out why that wouldn't work, I realised that it would. Why had I never thought of that? Now he was grinning at me, his annoying face full of knowing superiority. 'I need to get more rings,' I murmured, turning my attention back to the pan so I could complete this spell. It was primed, so I turned all the water to superheated steam, leaving the blood behind in the amulet and said 'Cordus' to complete it. To answer his curious look, I said, 'I have to pick a word I will not accidentally say in public. If I used the word *mouse* and said it in conversation at the deli counter, everyone standing in front of me would get blasted through the air.'

'That's a reasonable safety precaution,' he acknowledged.

I blew out my breath as I tried to get the ring on my finger. Waving it in the air had cooled it to the point where it wouldn't burn my skin, but my hope that it would have expanded enough with the heat for me to get it on just wasn't happening.

'Tape it in place?' the werewolf suggested, once again coming up with a practical solution I just hadn't considered.

Settling in to watch me, the werewolf found a tub of ice cream in the freezer, sat himself on the counter across from the hob, and worked his way through the whole thing, spoon after spoon until two litres of it were gone.

Thirty minutes later, I had ten tiny rings taped to my fingers with sticking plaster. I looked a bit odd, but I had ten shots at deflecting an attack, and that might come in very handy soon.

'What's next?' he asked.

'To eat?' I replied mockingly.

He patted his belly; a flat, taut wall of muscle. 'I think I'm okay for now. Aren't there some women we are supposed to be finding? This is all very nice, but I figure we are going to get found here soon and unless you are keeping secrets from me,' he eyed me deliberately to make sure I knew that would be a bad idea, 'you still don't know how to get us home.'

He was right. It was time to get on with the final stage. I had to use up some time to make sure I was ready, or we would be charging in half-cocked, but there was no excuse for delaying any further. Heike was here somewhere. I just hoped she and Katja were in the same place because I had no way of finding Katja unless I went back to our realm, got her sweater, came back here … I didn't want to contemplate it.

Using a barbeque skewer I found in the kitchen and some more of the sticky tape, I attached the triangular piece of bunting to it and then skewered Heike's bank card. It wasn't the same as a piece of clothing, but it was something she would have touched a lot, every day even, so it would carry a sense of her, and that was all I needed.

It went onto the lawn outside the house as I conjured an air spell to guide me. Instantly the makeshift flag fluttered in one direction only. This told me two things: firstly, that the spell had worked and the bank card contained a clear echo of its owner, and secondly, that she wasn't too far away.

'Ready?' I asked my large friend.

'Nope.' I thought he was being flippant for a moment, but he dropped the sword point down into the lawn and went back inside the house. When he re-emerged more than a minute later, he saw my bemused expression. 'What?' he asked as he picked up the sword. 'Everyone has to go to the bathroom sometime.'

'Ready now?' I asked, doing my best to keep the sarcasm from my tone.

He said, 'Um ...' but he was just teasing me this time, setting off across the lawn in the direction the flag had shown while shouting, 'It's hero time. Last one to die is a wimpy wizard.'

Chapter 21

Trekking cross country, I couldn't shake the feeling that we were on Earth, and maybe we were, but just a different version of it. Everything about it was the same. After the sun set and the stars appeared, I could work out if we were still in the same astral position. Or at least I could if I knew any star patterns, which I didn't.

I asked the werewolf about it, thinking he must look at the moon all the time, but he just gave me a look that told me I was being ridiculous.

The grass was the same, the trees were the same; hell, it even smelled the same. There was no litter though; that was one thing. Another, when I started to look for incongruities, was the lack of aircraft. Once I noticed that, I wondered why I couldn't hear any traffic. We were in the countryside, so it could be that we are just a long way from the nearest autobahn, but there were no sounds at all that could not be attributed to nature.

No sound anywhere to disturb the tranquillity of the open fields.

It was as if all the people were missing.

Every hundred metres or so, I paused to repeat the tracking spell, adjusting our trajectory each time to keep us on track. The first signal suggested she was close, but close is a relative thing.

An hour passed, or what I thought was an hour, as we trekked through the open countryside, following the wind. I should have taken a watch from the house. It hadn't occurred to me, but it was one-thirty in the afternoon when we left and had to be coming up on three now. If this realm operated like Earth, in an hour, it would begin to get dark and the sun would set quickly once it got started.

The werewolf was still wearing the pants and shirt he had on in the cell block. One of the penalties of his size was the limited likelihood of finding anything to fit him. He hadn't even bothered trying at Daniel's house. I didn't ask him if he were cold. If he was, he showed no sign plus asking him would only highlight his predicament and earn me a snark-fuelled comment.

'Where are the roads, wizard?' It was the first time he had spoken in an hour. He was always alert, always looking to the distance but he didn't display any animalistic behaviour like sniffing the air. I couldn't tell if my expectations were just silly stereotypes from films and books about werewolves; they were my only frame of reference. Whatever the case, he acted like anyone else, but with an edge of training.

Then it hit me. 'Were you a solider?'

'I asked my question first, wizard,' his grumbling reply came back. 'My feet are starting to get cold, and the wet can be a problem if it goes on too long.'

'I don't know if there are any roads. All I can do is follow the tracking spell. I expected to have reached her by now.'

'Perhaps that's it over there.' He nodded with his head, making me squint.

'I don't see anything.'

'That's because you are so short, tiny wizard. You'll see it in a minute.' He was right. As we continued up the slight rise we were climbing, a building emerged in the distance. It was mostly hidden in the trees, but it was wide and squat and built of red bricks. It looked like a farm building.

I paused, crouching to perform the spell one last time and got the strongest indication yet: we had found Heike's location. What now, though? Back home, I might call for back up and that was not an option here. Having said that, back home I might assume

I could handle whoever was inside with the missing person, and that *really* wasn't a safe assumption to make here.

The werewolf knelt next to me, using one hand with his finger extended to point in the same direction as the flag. 'That's it? She's in there?' he asked.

'Ninety-nine percent certain.'

He frowned into the distance, thinking. 'We should wait until dark. You can't see that far with your special sight, can you?'

'Second sight,' I corrected him though I suspected he got it wrong on purpose. 'No, I can't. I would need to get a lot closer in order to tell if there was anyone … hostile inside. I think it likely we will encounter resistance, but I cannot predict how many or how powerful they might be.'

'Have you fought a demon yet?'

'Nope.'

'Do you think they will be strong?' he asked.

I sucked on my lips as I nodded. 'I think the one we know as Daniel keeps the wizard that took Heike as a familiar.'

'But you fought the wizard?'

'Twice.'

'How'd that go?'

'Got my butt kicked.'

He pursed his lips. 'How'd it go the second time?'

'Same as the first.'

'Wizard, you really suck, you know that?'

I couldn't put up much of an argument. Turning my head to look for the sun, I found it was nearing the horizon and twilight was creeping across the countryside. 'I think we are right to wait. They only go to Earth at night. I don't know if they can only go at night or if they do it by choice. However, if night is their time to be somewhere else, it might diminish the numbers here.'

The werewolf placed his sword and assault rifle on the ground, followed them down, turned over and breathed out a big sigh. 'That would be a big help if we knew how many we were up against to start with. Wake me up when it is time to go.'

Chapter 22

I waited until I was happy that it was fully dark and then waited another half an hour. I didn't have to question whether the werewolf was asleep or not because I could have heard his snoring from Bremen.

He wasn't easy to wake either, my gentle tapping getting completely ignored and my more insistent shaking managing only to elicit a waft from one sleepy arm. I briefly considered hitting him with a lightning spell but dismissed it in case he woke up discombobulated and tried to kill me. Instead, I licked my finger and shoved it in his ear.

That worked.

'What the f...?' He sprang to his feet and spun around to face me, holding his head on one side as he wriggled a finger around inside his ear to dry it out. 'That better have been your finger, wizard. I was having a perfectly good dream about a waitress I met once.'

'I don't need any details, thank you.' There were no lights on in the building ahead, so it was now impossible to discern it from the murky blackness of everything else. The sky was mostly clear, allowing a gibbous moon to illuminate the countryside not hidden under a canopy of trees. 'How good is your night sight?' I asked, wondering if this was where his animal nature might provide something useful.

'Perfect,' he replied. 'When I change, that is. Right now, I can see only what the moon shows.'

Helpful.

UNTETHERED MAGIC

A question occurred to me, 'When you change, is it still you?' He looked at me with his top lip curled in question. 'I mean, are you a fully berserk, kill everything in sight werewolf like in *An American Werewolf in London*? Or are you in control and still thinking clear thoughts like Alcide from *True Blood*?'

'The latter. Don't worry; we're not going to find the ladies just so I can eat them. I can't very easily use the weapons once I change though so I'll be holding off for now. I'll transform when I need to.' I didn't question it, but I couldn't see why he would need the weapons if he was a mighty, giant werewolf.

We set off, making a beeline for some trees that would mask our approach. Keeping them close to our left, we came down the incline toward the farm building we knew was hidden in the trees. I had an air spell prepared, both hands ready to throw it at the first sign of trouble, but my mind was ready to switch to earth or water or whatever if I needed something more destructive. I wasn't worried about hurting whoever we found to be holding the women, but fire and lightning would give our position away and ruin my night vision very quickly. Earth was a conjuring I tended to avoid, simply because it was so destructive. Out here in the countryside, in a realm that looked like Earth but wasn't, I didn't care two bits if I caused an earthquake with my efforts.

My second sight, which would show me ley lines and supernatural creatures, didn't do anything about the dark, so I had to hope I could see well enough to not trip over or fall down a hole.

Getting closer, we realised that there simply wasn't any light to see at the farm building. I thought perhaps it was just the case that there were no windows on this side, but the whole area was a blanket of darkness. Would there be sentries posted? Up on the hill, I had watched and listened while the werewolf slept, but had seen and heard no one. The tracking spell told me Heike was there still, and finally, I was close enough to see the misty gold outline of a supernatural creature. It was inside the building, but it wasn't alone.

I placed my hand gently on my partner's shoulder so he would stop. Then, getting close to his ear, I whispered, 'I can see them inside. I just can't tell what they are from here. It might be shilts, it could be demons.'

I heard him exhale through his nose. 'After I finish kicking them in the balls, I'll ask them. Any sign of the women?'

'I can't pick up human signatures, just those of creatures that use ley line energy. Or, at least, I think that's what I see. It is the same colour ...'

'Yeah, yeah, yeah, wizard. You're boring me. Let's find a door and introduce ourselves.' He didn't wait for me to answer; we were thirty metres from the building and coming around the edge of some more trees so we would be in shadow and effectively invisible.

Effectively invisible isn't the same thing as actually invisible though and we had been spotted some time ago.

The attack, when it came, was sudden and unexpected. I could see magical auras even through buildings, but apparently not through trees. Suddenly, there were dozens of them coming at us. The darkness made it confusing, but the werewolf reacted less than half a second after the first of them rushed us. His big gun barked, spitting bullets at an insane rate and making my ears ring after the hours of utter silence.

They came from all sides, and we found ourselves back to back so I couldn't tell how effective he was, but I had my own front to defend and an arsenal to try out. This was going to be my first fight without my missing wand, and I was genuinely just as excited as I was terrified.

The first wave came silently, but after my readied air spell knocked them back, they abandoned their stealth and ran at us, screaming war cries as they came. It was shilt; no disguise this time, they were wearing their true features with pride. However, it wasn't only shilt; there was something else. In the darkness, a shadow whipped by at ground level running on all fours like a dog.

Well, stand by fellas, because you're about to get both barrels.

They were all around us, cutting off any escape route, but that just made it easy to hit them. I went with fire, drawing ley line energy directly from the earth to feed the outrushing energy. Without my wand to focus the jet, it came out looking and feeling more ragged, but it was also more powerful. As it lit the night and ruined my night vision, it showed me targets; the first of which lifted his small sword to parry the fire as they always do. I expected to have to switch to a different technique, but the fire drove him back.

It was too powerful for him to deflect. Suddenly, he was on fire, and I was switching my aim to hit another.

Behind me, the weapon stopped firing. 'I'm out,' the werewolf shouted in his deep bass grumble. 'Can you hold them off?'

I wanted to ask why, but there was no time for a Q and A session, the shilt were attacking in vast numbers; there had to be dozens of them. Several were on fire, but still they came, and I knew their numbers would prove too great soon enough. Picking them off one at a time was a poor tactic.

I threw an air spell in and set it loose, so it hit everything around us in a complete circle, like a bomb blast going off to expand outwards in every direction. I bought me the few seconds I needed to agitate the moisture in the air.

'Get down!' I yelled when it reached critical point, releasing the lightning from a fist held above my head so the lightning flashed and arced in every direction. It was blinding, especially so close with my irises wide in the dark. I turned my head away instinctively, which exposed me to attack, and I got to find out what the dark dog-like shapes were.

I turned my head away instinctively which exposed me to attack as two of the devil dogs hit my midriff, their snarling teeth coming for my face. They had leathery skin where they ought to have fur and their heads were hard and smooth like a bone. A third bit my left arm as it flailed, stopping me from getting up. With them on top of me, I couldn't even use my defensive amulets as the dogs would be safe inside the barrier with me.

I could pull a spell into my right hand, but I was using that to defend my head. I was ugly enough without having a devil dog rip half of it off. I cried out in pain as simultaneously the dogs bit my right and left arms, their teeth going through my layers of clothing to pierce the flesh beneath. If I didn't get up soon, the shilt would be upon me, and that would be game over.

'Will you stop messing about?' The grumbling voice of the werewolf reached my ears just as two of the dogs were ripped away from me. A dog-like yelp vanished into the distance as he threw them back at the shilt standing all around us, their faces illuminated by a fire now started in the branches of several trees.

I was looking at them from the ground, scrambling to get up to defend myself but they had stopped mid-attack and none of them were looking at me. Their eyes were trained on a spot a metre above me and I found out why when I glanced up.

My partner had stripped off and transformed. That was why he asked if I could hold them off; he needed a moment to perform the shift.

The werewolf was standing over me, ragged breaths huffing in and out as if he was psyched up and about to let rip. He was taller, I realised, as I gained my feet, now standing close to two and a half meters tall, but height wasn't what had stopped the shilt. The werewolf stood on its back legs like a man and was man-shaped with the exception of its head. He was muscular as a man, but all of that had been amplified, lumps and bumps tiering from its neck down over its arms and torso. His white Caucasian skin was matte black now and covered in sparse but coarse black hair. Light glowed in lines all over his body as if he had liquid gold flowing through his veins and I understood now why he didn't want to transform earlier; it would have given our approach away. At the end of his arms, huge claws that looked like knives reflected light from the fires and his eyes were mad. But all of that paled into comparison with the horror that was his mouth.

His lips were pulled back to show a row of teeth that would scare a shark. I cannot tell you how glad I was that he was on my side.

'What's the matter?' he asked the shilt. 'Never seen a werewolf before?' Then he looked down at me and tutted. 'If you feel like helping out, any time would do.' I was just standing there, staring at him like everyone else. Had he not jolted me back to my senses I would have kept on staring too.

As a guttural growl that started somewhere deep in his soul escaped from his clenched teeth, I threw off the pain I felt from my wounds, roared my own defiance and dug deep into the earth to pull at it.

Like I said before, earth spells are not something I have conjured very often, simply because they are so destructive. In this environment, all bets were off.

The werewolf took off, tensing his back legs before leaping forward into the melee of shilt and devil dogs. I wanted to watch, but I was exposed on every side and about to get attacked. Throwing caution to the wind, I dropped both hands, using my left as well as my right to tear into the soil and rock beneath me. I could feel ten metres down into the ground, which I felt certain was more than enough. The shilt were coming again, enough of them to overpower me easily.

I let them get closer, their swords up to cut me down when they got within range and the devil dogs charging again, dozens of them coming all at once as if sensing they had a shot to take me out now. I checked where the werewolf was, then released the spell, line energy ripping through my body to power it as I ripped out a donut of ground all around me. It was ten metres across and left just a one-metre lump in the middle where I stood. In one move, it turned the whole thing over on itself, burying dozens of shilt and dogs three metres deep below the soil.

Suddenly, all was still but for the enraged and terrible sounds from the werewolf and shouts from the shilt as they tried to escape. He was standing on his legs (though I wanted to call them back legs) and slicing into the shilt as if they were nothing. He locked eyes with me. 'You couldn't have done that sooner, huh?'

He muttered something that sounded like useless something wizard and bounded into the dark chasing more shilt as they ran from him.

Somebody slow clapping got my attention.

'Well done, Otto. Well done.'

Chapter 23

Illuminated by the dancing light of the fire in the trees and bushes, the wizard stepped out. He was still wearing his elegant waistcoat and trousers, the chain leading to his pocket watch catching the light as he moved. He nodded to his left and to his right, telling the shilt to wait.

'It seems I underestimated your skill, dear fellow. That was actually quite impressive, and I see you have dispensed with that ridiculous wand. It was stifling your power.'

'Yes. I had not realised that until I was forced to work without it.'

He nodded, glancing down to check his footing as he advanced to the edge of the ring of turned earth. 'You brought a friend with you too, I see. He is quite the brutish specimen though I cannot see a use for him here. I imagine they will just kill him. You, on the other hand, might now attract a demon of power.'

'I have no plan to stay, thank you. I came for the woman you took. She is inside that building, yes?'

He raised his eyebrows in surprise; perhaps tracking spells weren't a thing here. 'She is. I would say well done again, but then I would be repeating myself and it would be redundant anyway because you are trapped here.' He paused, checking the ground again before fixing me with a curious look. 'You are trapped here, yes? You haven't somehow become the first human ever to learn how to move between the immortal and mortal realms? That would be quite the trick actually and one which might convince me to let you go if you were to show me it.'

UNTETHERED MAGIC

He was talking and filling in some of the many, many blanks I had. What I didn't know was whether he was talking so he could stall me while others got into attack position. I glanced around but no one was moving. The shilt were still there, forming a sparse circle around me now that their numbers were vastly depleted, and they did not seem inclined to attack. I was happy to talk for now. Maybe I would fare better in a third fight with this chap and maybe I wouldn't, but I would rather have the missing werewolf return to give me a hand before the fight started if possible.

'Perhaps we should get acquainted. My name is Otto Schneider, but I think you already know that.'

He bowed from the waist elegantly, splaying his arms as he dipped his head. 'Edward Blake at your service, sir. I am familiar to Daniel, a position I fought initially but one which has given me power and recognition. When the death curse fails, I will be released and have my own power in the new world.'

'The death curse. You mentioned that before. Please tell me about it and what it means.'

He smiled and flipped his eyebrows. 'No, I don't think so. I don't want to spoil the surprise. Humanity will find out soon enough, I can assure you. Enough idle chatter now. Can you move between realms?'

He was trying to push us on, but I had too many questions to be rushed. 'You speak of realms. The mortal and immortal you called them. If you tell me what I don't know, I will reveal my secret.'

'Enough!' he snapped. 'You are no match for me. I have extended you the courtesy of not killing you twice already. This time I will make you beg for mercy, and then I will take your secrets whether you wish to give them to me or not. Then Daniel can advance himself a little more by handing you to whomever he pleases.'

Time for talk was clearly over; the familiar feeling of ley line energy being drawn filled my senses as Edward prepared to attack. The werewolf was still nowhere in sight, but there was no time to consider him now. I was on my own, up against a man that had already kicked my butt twice in as many days, and I was surrounded by his allies.

He threw fire at me first, a roaring wall of flame that startled me even though I told myself to be ready for it. Instinctively, I said, 'Cordus' to activate the first of my defensive spells. The shield wall came up and stopped the flame from reaching me, but I felt singed from the heat of it, such was its power. He held the flame on me, pouring more and more energy into it in an attempt to overwhelm. In response, I threw water at him, pulling it in from the air and the ground, muddying his clothes but doing little more than annoying him even though it doused his flame just as my barrier flickered and died.

I could see the rage in his eyes as his next spell leapt from his hands, but I had one of my own; lightning to match his lightning, the arcs striking each other in the ten-metre space between us. The effect was spectacular, an explosion of light and raw power that channelled into the earth, the sky, and the trees where it started yet another fire. The shilt standing too close got it as well, screams of surprise from those affected as it tore through them.

I maintained the lightning for as long as I could, forcing more and more particles to collide feverishly above and around me. I felt like I was standing at ground zero, the centre of a swirling maelstrom of potential death, and it was hard to control.

Still the lightning arced and flashed, both of us trying to beat the other back but neither finding a way through. Light from the fires burning around us, combined with the flashes of lightning, distorted his features, making him look horrific, but the effect was like watching a strobe, intermittent images appearing and disappearing. My jaw began to hurt from gritting my teeth and my arms and legs were beginning to shake from the effort. In contrast, my opponent looked fresh and filled with vigour.

Knowing I couldn't hold the lightning on him for much longer, I prepared to switch tactics. He acted first though, dropping the lightning with a final flourish to push me off balance, then conjuring an earth spell that sent a ripple across the ground like someone flicking one end of a sheet to create a wave.

In the dark, I failed to see it coming until it lifted my feet from the ground. I fell backward, losing my focus, and the fire spell I had been about to throw escaped me as my hands went out to stop me eating dirt. He was on me instantly, my defences failing as I tumbled and tried to get back to my feet. He glimpsed the opening and this time when he threw lightning my way, it hit its target.

The strike threw me across the clearing, hurling me into the air like I'd trod on a landmine. Simultaneously, every cell in my body screamed in protest at the flare of white-hot electricity trying to find a way to earth. He could have finished me there and then, conjuring fire would have burned me to death before I could get a barrier up, conjuring the earth could have buried me. Or he might have chosen to create a tornado of air and water to drown me as I spun inside it.

He did none of those things though. He waited for me to get up, calmly brushing some marks from his waistcoat until he accepted that it was ruined and gave up. 'I haven't been able to test myself for a long time, Otto. Thank you for being a worthwhile opponent. With training you might even be able to best me. It is shame you will not accept your position and surrender. Perhaps you would like one last chance to reconsider?'

In his hands he readied an air spell. If I refused his offer, he would attack again, driving me back and beating me down again and again until he grew bored and killed me. Where the hell was the stupid werewolf? I clambered painfully to my feet as he began to whip the air into a storm. He was combining spells! I had never seen this before. Lying in bed at night and thinking about how I use my magic and what I might be able to do with it, I had wondered if something like this might be possible, but had never believed it was possible to pull it off. Now I was witnessing it.

Above his right hand and extending into the sky to a height of thirty metres, a roiling ball of water droplets, spinning air currents and barely contained lightning flashed and arced. It was a miniature thunderstorm at his command, and he was going to kill me with it.

'Surrender!' his voice boomed across the clearing.

I blew out a hard breath to steel myself and raised both hands in defiance. I wasn't going out without a fight, and I had one shot left that he might not be expecting.

Seeing that I was readying a spell of my own, he growled his disappointment, 'Fool.' Then he let the storm go. It flew across the divide, racing toward me with all the power and destruction inside it ready to unleash on yours truly. I threw an air spell to push it back and lifted a defensive barrier by activating the next ring with a new code word, 'Dancer.' The storm hit my spell, and though it slowed, it wasn't going to stop; there was just too much power, energy, and inertia.

I was watching my opponent, all my focus on him as I waited for him to do the thing that might save me. The storm came on, inexorably drawing closer even as I tried to push it back. I had seconds left before the storm would reach me. At that point, my barrier would be severely tested. I didn't think it would hold for long against the storm heading my way, but I was ready to drop it and expose myself because that was the key to winning.

Then it happened. Whether he grew bored of my resistance or believed he was able to end this instantly using his superior skill, he did what I hoped he would and reached out with his magic to grasp my air spell. He had done it successfully twice before and I had tried to work out how to perform that trick with no success of my own. Which was why when he did it this time, I dropped the spell instantly.

With no barrier pushing against it, the storm surged forward. I had seconds until it devoured me, but I conjured a new air spell, this one coming from behind Edward to propel him forward just as he tried to pull my previous air spell his way. He grabbed thin air and pitched forward just as the airwave from behind picked him up to fling him forward. He was coming right for me, flying through the air uncontrollably as I caught him by surprise. There was too little time for him to react, so he collided with his own storm spell even as he tried to pull back the magic sustaining it.

The storm fell apart without his magic keeping it alive, but not fast enough for him to avoid its effects. Lightning hit him, as dirt, ice and water particles contained in the wind tore at his skin, flaying him while he fell to the ground. He was coming straight for me and would have collided with my defensive barrier, but as our eyes locked and I saw the hatred behind them still, I dropped that too, reaching to my belt and the weapon I took from the task force soldier in Berlin.

In one smooth move, as Edward fell the final metre to collide with me, I lunged forward and hit him with the stun gun, unloading the weapon's charge directly into his chest. He juddered as it flowed through him to the ground but fell backward away from me as he lost consciousness.

For a moment, I stood panting with the spent taser still in my hand, unable to believe I had won; the wizard laying defeated at my feet.

'That was cool, man.' The werewolf's voice suddenly breaking the silence scared the crap out of me, making me jump on the spot as I swung around to see where the noise had come from.

'Were you seriously watching that?' I asked incredulously. 'You didn't think maybe I could do with a hand?'

He stepped out of the shadows. 'You didn't need a hand. You won, quite clearly demonstrating that you didn't need me. Maybe helping would have not helped at all. Besides, that would have robbed you of the knowledge that you could beat him.' His attention switched away from me to my right. 'Hold on a second.' He bounded away, screams from shilts echoing back out from the trees a few seconds later.

By the time he emerged again, wiping dark liquid from his jaws, I hadn't moved. I felt spent, but there was still much to do. 'Did you kill them all?' I asked.

'Goodness, no.'

'Really?' I frowned at him with disbelief.

'They're actually quite cool guys when you get to know them. Some of them have a bridge club; we were just discussing when to get together.'

He was a snarky dickhead. 'Okay, so they're all dead. You need to keep at least one alive, so we can get out of here. Had you thought of that?'

'I had not,' he admitted. Arriving next to me, he kicked the unconscious wizard in the head lightly to see what he did. The answer was nothing, even when he kicked him again a little harder. 'What do you want to do with him?'

'We have to take him back. He cannot be allowed to continue terrorising Bremen or anywhere else.'

Expressions were less easy to read on his werewolf face, but I was fairly sure he was showing me disbelief. 'We don't know how we are getting back yet, we still haven't found the ladies, and we need to carry him and keep him unconscious because the moment he comes around, he is going to try to stick a lightning bolt up our butts. Had you thought of that?'

Tipping my head as I conceded the point, I repeated his words, 'I had not.'

The werewolf turned around and strode a few paces away to bend and pick something up off the floor. It was clumsy in his big wolf hands, the sword now looking tiny and out of place as he tried to grip it.

I put my hands up to stop him. 'Whoa, big fella. We can't just kill him.'

'Why the hell not? He was going to kill you. Besides, I heard him call me a brute. I feel offended and demand satisfaction.' I had to physically get in his way as he advanced with the sword. Everything he said made sense, but I wasn't content to end a life just because the person was perceived as dangerous.

Edward's scream of defiance changed that instantly as the werewolf and I realised neither of us had been watching him and he was back on his feet. As he straightened up to his full height, pulling ley line energy into each of his hands, I went for a fire spell and hoped he was weakened.

I didn't get to find out how much power he had left because the sword buried itself in Edward's chest, the werewolf electing to throw it like a javelin. The wizard's mouth formed a surprised O shape as the spells died in his hands and he looked down to the hilt of the sword sticking out of his ribcage. He looked back up at me and then fell backward to the ground where I was sure, this time, he would stay.

'Yay!' whooped the werewolf, doing a running man dance on the spot like he had just scored a touchdown.

Forcing myself to ignore the aches, wounds, stiffness, and fatigue, I stooped to check the wizard's pulse. He was quite dead. At least it wasn't me that killed him.

As the werewolf drew the sword back out, wiping the blood on the wizard's clothing to clean it, I stood up and took a deep breath. My second sight showed no other creatures anywhere in sight. If there were any shilt or devil dogs left alive, they had already fled, but that might mean reinforcements were arriving, so time was still not our friend.

'We need to find Heike and Katja.'

Chapter 24

With no one left to oppose us, we walked to the building and then around it to find a door. It was locked, but that wasn't going to stop me for long. I pulled moisture from the air, knowing I could use it to freeze the lock and force it to burst, but the werewolf kicked the door off its hinges first.

'After you,' he said with a graceful sweeping bow.

It was dark inside, but the brick-built structure had no windows to let light in, and the shaft of moonlight from the door barely lit anything. 'You can see, right?' I asked the werewolf.

'Like it was day. I can smell too, and there are people in here: sweat, aftershave, blood. There's more than just a girl and a woman in here.'

I conjured fire, holding a flame above my hand to illuminate the passageway before us as best as I could. We didn't have to go far; the people inside could hear us coming. They were trying to be quiet, which inevitably led to them making insistent hushing noises. There being no background noise whatsoever; we found them easily.

Yet again, they were behind a locked door. I called out, 'Heike, it's Otto. Are you there?'

There was a brief pause before a familiar voice answered, 'Otto?'

Bingo! I had her.

Through the door, she asked, 'Otto, how did you find me?'

I stepped to the side, calling out, 'Stand back. We're going to open the door.' I offered my tall, hairy friend the opportunity to show off his strength again. 'Go ahead, big bad wolf, it's huff and puff time.'

'Ha, ha, wizard.' He took one step back, stepped forward again as he lifted his right leg and thrust it forward just as Heike opened the door. The werewolf let out a girlish squeal of surprise as he performed a close approximation of the splits and everyone inside screamed as the giant animal landed in the middle of their group.

I jumped over him. 'It's okay! It's okay! He's with me. We came to get you out.'

The screaming didn't exactly stop though, not helped when the werewolf turned to face everyone, showing them his teeth in what I think was supposed to be a friendly smile.

'Can you cut that out?' I begged.

He tried a pinky wave instead, saying, 'Sorry,' as he did, which seemed to finally calm the crowd.

A middle-aged woman said, 'That is literally the scariest thing I have ever seen.'

The werewolf smiled again. 'Thank you.'

Then, remembering that Heike opened the door, I asked, 'Wasn't it locked?'

She pulled me into a hug, held me for a second, then patted my back in thanks and let me go again. 'It was locked from the inside,' she explained. 'They didn't bother to lock it because they knew we couldn't escape. There were dozens of those shilt things. Maybe even a hundred, plus these awful doglike creatures they call gindars and the chap you fought at the morgue. We locked it from the inside to make us feel a little safer. Not that it would make much difference because they could just kick it in like your big dog tried to do.'

'Big dog?'

Heike said, 'Sorry. I'm not sure what you are.'

The werewolf stood up to his full two and a half metre height and looked down at himself. 'I'm a werewolf,' he said as if it was perfectly obvious. 'I'll be outside. There's no room in here.' As he wandered back along the passageway, we could all hear him muttering, 'Big dog? I ask you.'

In the room, now that I looked, were a dozen people. Men and women, almost an even split and a mix of ages from late teens up to a man in his fifties. They looked dishevelled and dirty but not injured or in need of medical assistance.

I said, 'Come on, we have to get out of here.'

'Can you get us home?' the older man asked.

The honest answer was no, but I wasn't going to tell them that. 'Yes,' I lied. 'But not by myself. To get here, we had to capture a shilt. If we can do that again, getting home will be easy.'

'Was all that noise outside you?' asked Heike, sticking close to me as we left the building.

'Yes, the shilt wanted to fight us, and then Edward turned up. It was … challenging, shall we say.'

'You're alright, though?'

I didn't get a chance to answer because there were other questions. 'How are you going to get us home?' and, 'Where's Daniel? Are we safe from him now?' then, 'Did you beat the wizard? What does that make you?'

I had to pick one to answer but chose instead to ask one of my own. 'Do you know why you are here?' They all started talking at once, and I had to hold up my hands to quiet them down. 'Just one, please.' I pointed to a young man; he was wearing a cop uniform I realised. 'You're Officer Nieswand.'

'I am.' He thrust his hand out to shake. 'Klaus Nieswand. That Edward guy hit me with something when the shilts attacked. I woke up here. I think it has something to do with magic. That's what Daniel said.'

'That's right,' agreed the middle-aged woman who didn't like the werewolf. 'He told me I would be a useful familiar if I could learn to control my inner abilities. I told him I had no idea what he was talking about.'

I looked at my audience, all their eyes focused on me. 'You were all brought here because you can do magic?'

'I wasn't,' answered Heike. 'I was brought here to lure you. I guess it worked but not the way they wanted if you beat them.'

'Did you beat Daniel?' Officer Nieswand asked.

I shook my head. 'I haven't met him yet,' I admitted. 'He is ... was Edward's boss?'

'His owner, I think,' said Heike. 'It was hard to work out the relationship. Daniel came across as some kind of powerbroker. He talked about status and who he could gain favour with by providing them with a trained familiar. I think he intended to have Edward hone some kind of magical ability within the people he took and then pass them on for his own benefit.'

It sounded like slave trading to me. Find people in the mortal realm with some natural magical ability, snatch them, train them so they can be of use and then pass them on to influential figures for whatever benefit he believes he can gain.

'Hold on,' my pulse quickened as I realised what I wasn't seeing, 'where's Katja Weber?'

'Daniel took her last night,' said a young woman standing in the middle of the crowd. She was in her teens just like Katja, their similar age and gender undoubtedly causing them to bond in the extreme environment. She was hugging herself and looking both cold and terrified. 'I think she was more attuned to her abilities than any of the rest of us. She could make things move. It wasn't much, but I thought I imagined it the few times when I did anything.'

I really wanted to explore what all these people could do, but I had to find the girl I came here for.

Just then, a sound brought my focus up, adrenalin charging my senses as I swung around to face the new danger. It was the werewolf though, returning through the trees and foliage carrying something in his left hand. In the darkness, I hadn't realised he had left us.

People spread out so he could come into the middle of the group whereupon we saw the thing he carried like a rag doll was a shilt. He had it by a foot and was bumping its head along the ground quite deliberately.

'You lot were all nattering, so I figured I would see if there were any of these little beasties left alive. This one was sticking out of the earth where you turned it all over. I'm sure he would very much like to open a portal for us. Isn't that right, Bob?'

'His name's Bob?' asked Heike, sounding surprised because she didn't know what the werewolf was like.

'Yeah,' he replied. 'Well, I named him actually. But, I figure, since he is going to do us all a solid and help us get home, he really deserves a name to go by.' I had to wonder what a shrink would make of the werewolf; the contents of his head were a kaleidoscope of weird bumping eternally into daft or just plain stupid.

Looking down at the upended shilt, I said, 'We can send them home, but we have to stay. Katja Weber was taken already.'

'By whom,' he growled, back to serious instantly.

I looked at the group. It was the teenage woman that answered. 'She was being given to a demon called Teague. Daniel acted as if it was a big honour and was going to be great for her.' She started crying. 'She begged him to leave her alone, but he didn't care what she wanted.'

I tilted my head so I could focus on the upside-down shilt's face. 'Do you know where Teague lives?' I got no answer.

The werewolf gave Bob the shilt a shake. 'Hey, Bob. I thought we had a deal.' He sounded friendly like a car salesman, disappointment in his voice now because the customer was backing out.

I tried asking the question again but stopped myself because my neck was getting sore. 'Can you turn him up the right way?'

'Sure.' The werewolf threw Bob into the air and spun him, catching him by his neck before he could land.

Now that I could look directly at him, I tried using reason. 'We can kill you right now. It would be very easy for my big friend, but you can survive this. Open a portal to the mortal world in Bremen, send these people home and then take us to Teague's house and we will let you go.'

'No, you won't,' it hissed in reply.

'Yes, I will,' argued the werewolf. 'Scout's honour.' He held up his spare hand in the scouts' salute.

Possibly he saw that he had no choice: die now or maybe die later, he moved his left hand, and a portal opened. There were joyous gasps from the group as they sensed home and escape was moments away. I touched the shilt's arm to make skin-to-skin contact and pushed my head through the shimmering air. The portal opened to reveal a familiar part of Bremen not far from the city centre.

I stepped back, making eye contact with Heike and then Nieswand and most of the others as I offered them the way home. 'It's safe.'

The middle-aged woman stepped up first. 'I left a pot on the stove when he came for me. My husband is way too stupid to have turned it off.'

Before she reached the shimmering air, another voice caused her feet to stop. 'How will you stop them coming for us again tomorrow? Daniel knows where to find us. He must have had some way of detecting whatever meagre ability we have. Won't we just end up back here?' The question was asked by the man in his fifties, and the joy of escape was instantly replaced by gasps of horror. Why bother escaping now if you were just going to be taken again tomorrow? What defence was there?

I huffed out a sigh. He was right. I just hadn't thought the problem through that far yet. Whatever else I did, I was going to have to fight Daniel and find a way to stop him coming to Earth.

'I want you all to go. Go home and be with your families. I don't have an answer for you yet. I am as in the dark as the rest of you, but I intend to find out. We were able to beat Edward. Maybe we can beat Daniel too.'

'And if you can't?' asked the older man.

'Then I'll most likely be dead, and I'm afraid there will be nothing more I can do to protect you.' My answer was honest. As honest as I could make it, but it still scared the group.

The older man said, 'Fair enough. I don't see how it's your responsibility to save us anyway.' Then he walked up to shake my hand, gripping it firmly between both of his. 'If I get just one more night at home with my Gertie, that will be gift enough. Thank you.' He let go of my hand, made contact with the shilt and stepped through the portal, stepping onto the street in Bremen and hugging himself against the even colder air that side.

Soon they were nearly all through. But I spotted the teenage woman about to take her turn and stopped her when I saw what she was wearing. 'Is that Katja's jacket?' I asked. I recognised it from a photograph in her room.

'Yes,' she said glumly. 'Do you think you can find her?'

I smiled as I nodded. 'I do now. Can I have it, please? I took off my ski jacket so she could use it to keep warm. Like the others, she wasn't dressed to be out in the winter air of Bremen at night, but she would survive as would they all.

Then there was just Heike and Officer Nieswand left. She walked with him to the shimmering air, then made like she was going to speak to me, let him get a pace ahead of her, and the moment he touched Bob's skin, she shoved him through. He made a surprised sound as he landed among the group on the cold street in Bremen, but Heike slapped Bob's left hand and the portal snapped shut.

'What the hell?' I asked.

Heike looked at me with a face that suggested I shouldn't waste my time arguing. 'I'm coming with you to get Katja.'

'No.'

'I didn't ask you for an opinion, Otto. She's a Bremen citizen, and I am a Bremen cop.'

'You're on suspension,' I countered. 'Go back to your family; you have no authority here. It's not like you can arrest Daniel.'

'I can try. He can come back to Bremen in cuffs and answer some questions. Maybe if we stick him in jail, he won't be able to snatch any more people.'

My eyebrows tried to touch my hairline. 'I don't think cuffs or jail cells will work on a demon. Not from what I have seen anyway.'

'Have you tried?' she asked.

I didn't bother answering her rhetorical question. 'Make him open the portal again,' I asked the werewolf.

'Don't do any such thing,' said Heike, still staring at me. 'I'm going with you, Otto. Stop wasting time and let's get this done.' Then, dismissing me and taking charge, she spoke to Bob, 'Can you take us to Teague's house? Can you use a portal thing to get us there?'

He sneered at her, 'It only goes between dimensions. To get there, you'll have to walk.'

'Will you lead us there?' she asked. He spat in her face, the werewolf lifting him up so he could look him in the eye as she fell back to wipe the disgusting liquid away.

'Now that wasn't very nice, was it, Bob?' the werewolf said. 'I think you should apologise to the lady and then show us how to get to where we need to go.'

The shilt swung a leg in an attempt to kick the werewolf. 'You can go fu…'

The werewolf flicked his arm and threw the shilt at a handy nearby tree where he made an impressive splat noise. By the time he landed in a broken heap at the base of the trunk, the werewolf had walked over to join me, calling, 'Bye, Bob,' over his shoulder.

'I thought you promised not to kill him, scout's honour.'

He sniggered and held a hand to his face in mock embarrassment. 'Don't tell anyone, but …' he checked around to see if anyone was listening, 'I was never in the scouts.'

'So, geniuses, what now?' asked Heike.

'Tracking spell?' the werewolf asked.

'Tracking spell,' I replied.

Chapter 25

Travelling to find Katja was the same process as finding Heike. I was irked that they hadn't been together; it would have made things neat and allowed me to finish the task and return to earth, or the mortal realm as I was now training myself to think of it.

We lived in the mortal realm, and now we were in the immortal realm, which suggested we ought to have a problem, but we had already killed dozens of shilt and gindars and Edward himself. So, what was the immortal thing all about? Concerned that I might find out soon and not like the answer, I kept my thoughts to myself.

The werewolf chose to stay in his werewolf form, stalking through the countryside beside Heike as I led the way. None of us had a watch to tell the time by, not that it really mattered because I didn't know if time here would move the same as on Earth or if we were in the same time zone. After being zapped by the deputy commissioner more than twenty-four hours ago, I had seen the time only once when we were in Daniel's house. My only thought on the subject was whether they could open a portal to the mortal realm once the sun came up. I would find out if we got that far. For now, at least, we were trapped here until we could find another shilt to open a portal for us.

Much like Daniel's place, the building we found as we closed in on Katja's signal was a grand country house. We had to scale a fence, which, for once, the werewolf didn't just rip down. Stealth was our friend now; we had no way of knowing if Teague was home until we got closer. He could be having a party with a houseful of demons for all I knew, celebrating his new familiar perhaps.

It was the middle of the night, and there were no lights on in the house. Katja was in there somewhere, the vastness of the house making me wish I had my trusty broken compass. It would have led me directly to her; the flag made of bunting was far less efficient.

First, we had to find a way in. 'Wolfman,' I called to get my nameless friend's attention.

'You call him wolfman?' asked Heike. 'Why don't you use his name?'

'Because he won't tell me and, unlike him, I'm not the creative type that instantly thinks to call someone Bob.'

She turned to look at the werewolf in the dark. 'Why won't you tell him your name?' she whispered.

He chuckled. 'Because it's way cooler being the wizard and the werewolf. Makes us sound like a rock band. Besides, not knowing is driving him nuts and there's no television, so I have to make my own entertainment.'

I could feel her staring at him with incredulous eyes. He was quite the character.

'Wolfman,' I tried again. 'We need a way in, but we don't want to wake anyone.'

'Yeah, I'm all about brute strength and smashing shit. You're the finesse guy. Can't you use air to pop a windowpane out or turn a key from the inside?'

Yet again, I was dumbfounded by how he came up with a simple solution when I couldn't. I didn't know if I could conjure an air spell delicate enough to turn a key, but I knew I could use flame to cut a hole.

Finding a set of patio doors with polyethylene panels below the glass above, I melted a small hole through and then worked along until I reached an edge. Making a turn, I cut three sides of a square and was about to cut the fourth when the werewolf put his sword down and got his claws under one edge. Then, he grunted slightly and peeled the panel back like opening a can of sardines. The hole was seven hundred millimetres in each direction; easily big enough for even the werewolf to fit through.

Inside, it looked like a house that a human family would live in. Remembering Daniel's place and the children's bedrooms, I couldn't shake the feeling that we were on a parallel version of Earth. Maybe that made sense; they talked about mortal and immortal realms, not different worlds. Perhaps this was Earth but shifted a little to the right somehow.

I gave Heike the flag to hold and tried the spell again. We were going to have to do that a lot if we were to find her in this huge house. Common sense told me she would be trapped in a basement or something, and when the flag pulled toward the carpet, I knew I was right.

'Basement?' whispered Heike.

'We need to find the stairs,' I replied, my voice just as quiet as hers.

Luck was with us as a random door in the first hallway we came to revealed a set of stairs leading down. It was dark, but Katja was down there somewhere. Hope was peeking its head above the parapets, daring to let me believe we might get her back. It would only leave one hurdle to overcome: how to get home. That was a problem for later, as was what to do about Daniel coming back for her the moment we got her to Earth.

'I'll wait here,' whispered the werewolf. 'Any attack will come this way, so I'll protect your rear. Get the girl and let's get out of here.'

I slapped his arm in thanks and headed down the stairs, Heike's hand on my shoulder for balance in the dark.

At the bottom, it was simply too dark to see, so I conjured flame into my right hand, the light instantly showing us the wretched girl in a cage in the corner.

She sobbed as she recognised Heike, the older woman rushing to the cage to offer the girl comfort. 'Don't worry, this is my friend. He killed Edward, and he's going to get us out of here. All the others are already back home.'

Heike was whispering, but Katja's wail of despair came out way too loud. Heike shoved a hand through the bars of the cage to clamp over her mouth, making shushing sounds all the while. The cage was a solid steel contraption, heavy enough on its own to not need to be bolted down and forming all six sides of a cube. A door with a padlock faced us.

'Stand back,' I whispered, but a sound like a blast of energy hitting a wall preceded a string of curse words from the werewolf.

Katja screamed in panic as flashes of light lit up the stairwell from above: The werewolf was fighting something, and my guess was Teague had awoken.

I rushed to help him, leaving Heike and Katja behind as the young woman screamed in protest to be set free of her cage. As I rushed up the stairs, I could see the shape of the werewolf ahead of me. There was no sign of his opponent or opponents, if indeed there was more than one up there, but as I neared the top step, a chunk of the wall exploded ahead of me, smashing into the werewolf to send him flying backwards. He shot from right to left as he passed in front of me and vanished out of sight.

I murmured, 'Prancer,' as my foot hit the top step, bringing my defensive shield up just in time to catch the next blast. I had no idea what it was, but the power of it shunted me sideways and burned my barrier out in one hit.

'Donner.' I didn't bother whispering this time, there was no need for stealth anymore, but as the fourth shield of the ten I had flashed into existence, I caught sight of Teague.

I figured that was who he was, even though I couldn't be certain. He was dressed in casual clothes, house slippers on his feet and a pair of wool-blend trousers with a cotton shirt and cardigan on top. He looked to be in his sixties, grey hair dominating with just a touch of the original brown left. A little overweight, he had a paunch that hung over his belt slightly. But what really drew my attention was the two glowing orbs of dark red he held in his hands.

He threw them both at me as one, the pair striking my shield to obliterate it.

'Vixen.' The next shield appeared, but he held off launching his next two orbs of death.

'Who are you?' he demanded.

'Just a guy hired by a woman to bring back her kidnapped daughter. You know, the one you have locked in a cage in the basement.'

He looked surprised. 'You are from the mortal realm?'

'Yes. If you'll be so kind as to open a portal, I'll take my friends and go back there right now. You can get back to sleep, or whatever it is you do at night around here.'

'The girl is mine. She is bonded to me,' he sneered. I wondered what he meant, but he extinguished the ball of glowing red in his right hand to reach up and pull his shirt to one side. Just above his heart, there was a tattoo or a brand or something on his skin. I wasn't sure what he was showing me, but it meant something.

'Well, I am taking her. I just killed Edward Blake; I'm sure killing you won't be much harder, old man.'

He laughed at me, a deep rumbling belly laugh because what I had said was so funny. 'I'm immortal, you fool. You call us demons, but that's just because your ancient memory of us is all twisted up. You can't kill me. I doubt you could even give me a headache. Edward Blake was Daniel's familiar; it's Daniel you should worry about. That pair have been together for nearly two hundred years. I'm tempted to let you run away so he can deal with you.'

I was looking around the room, wondering what I could use to test his immortal theory. He sounded pretty sure of himself though, and he had an orb in each hand again. He started stalking forward as I readied a spell in my right hand.

'How many of those barrier spells have you got?' he asked. 'A limited supply, I'm willing to bet. You draw on ley lines to provide your limited skills. There's a reason we have dominated the creatures of Earth since the dawn of time. We are the strongest, the only ones able to wield Earth's source energy. That inferior spell you are readying, whatever it is, will do nothing but annoy me. Go on. Give it your best shot, human.'

I couldn't believe it. He dropped both his arms and lifted his head to look directly upward so he wouldn't see what I was doing. The two glowing dark red orbs absorbed back into his hands, and he waited for me to throw my best shot.

Whatever confidence I might have felt was flowing away fast now, but there was nothing for it; I was going to have to do what I could.

Summoning fire, I shot a lance of it across the room. It engulfed the demon, setting fire to the carpet and the drapes and a couch positioned a few metres behind him. He screamed in pain, dancing back as his clothes and hair caught alight.

This was much more like it. Teague's overconfidence was his undoing. Immortal or not, he wasn't impervious to fire, and I had the upper hand. Keeping my barrier up because I had no idea what the red orbs might do to me, I focused the fire on him to drive him back.

He screamed in rage as he lifted his arms to fend the flame off. Crackling red light was arcing down his arms. I could see it flashing through the material of his clothing and when it reached his hands, it sparked and arced over his exposed skin even though it was on fire.

He pushed his palms together, fusing the two orbs into one which he then drew apart to create a far larger disc of energy. I tensed just before he fired it at me, but the blast picked me up and threw me back three meters to land on my butt as yet another defensive spell burnt out.

'Blitzen.' The next shield came up just in time to save me from the next ball of fizzing red death and was gone instantly. 'Comet.' Another to hide behind.

Teague had extinguished the fire on his clothes and skin, but his hair was gone, and his face was a mess, the outer layer of skin mostly burnt off. He seemed unconcerned about his injuries, as I might be with a papercut. As I picked myself up and willed myself to come up with something new I could try, a glowing green light came from his hands to envelop his body. Before my eyes, his skin began to heal. It gave me a chance to keep a barrier up for more than a few seconds, but he was going to be completely back to his starting condition if I didn't hit him again soon.

With the house around him on fire, the burning backdrop made him look like a creature from hell. The leering grin from a burnt face only added to the effect. I hit him with lightning, conscious that there was less power in it now than I had been able to conjure against Edward. I was flagging, and I knew it. My physical energy reserves would not last much longer.

He had to drop the healing spell to deal with the lightning, but to my great shame, he was able to reach out with a hand and catch it as it arced across the room. Like sucking a strand of spaghetti, the bolt of lightning just vanished into his palm. I crossed lightning from the list of options just as he threw two more glowing orbs at me, wrecking yet another shield.

I pushed air at him, creating a maelstrom in his room to hopefully confuse and bewilder him as I shouted, 'Rudolf,' and another shield, my seventh I thought, came up to defend me.

'Did you seriously use the reindeer names as your codewords?' asked the werewolf.

I glanced behind me, just as my barrier smashed again. 'Yes!' I shouted, ducking back into the next room. 'I thought they would be easy to remember, but I have three reindeer left, and I can't remember which ones.'

The werewolf was leaning against a wall, idly picking something from between his top row of fangs with a giant razor-sharp claw. 'I know I've said it already,' he said, spitting out whatever he had just worked loose. 'But you really are a bit crap, wizard.'

'Yes. I'm sure you're right. Now would you mind awfully if you help out a little with the enraged demon?'

'Werewolf to the rescue again, huh? I sure hope you got a few tricks left, because those red things he throws look like they will really sting.' Then he shoved off the wall with his shoulder, dived into the hallway and ducked under twin balls of death as he charged the demon, throwing the sword like a spear again. It might have worked last time, but Teague just swivelled like a boxer, so it sailed by to embed itself in a couch. It was just a distraction technique, though, as Teague looked back our way to find the werewolf right on him and swinging a clawed hand at his throat.

With the werewolf on Teague and drawing his attention, I conjured a water spell, seeking the liquid inside the demon and pulling at it. I sent heat to it, agitating the liquid as I pushed the temperature higher. I could feel Teague fighting against me, his attention divided as the werewolf tussled with him, trying to rip him apart. Slashing claws opened the demon's skin and shredded what remained of his clothing, but Teague, unable to react in time to form more hellfire, hit him with a spell that sent him spinning through the air.

The room was utterly destroyed already, and flames were licking at the ceiling, threatening to get out of hand if not dealt with soon and filling the room with smoke. I poured more energy into my spell, sensing that he would now turn his attention to me. My efforts were beginning to work, Teague was clearly struggling when he turned to face me this time. His skin was beginning to glow as the liquid inside it began to reach critical point. Any second now, it would hit the gaseous stage and I planned to hit him with lightning again to make him explode. Then we would see just how immortal he was.

'You can't kill me,' he screamed, his voice distorted by the pain I was inflicting. It had reached the point where he was unable to form fresh orbs to defend himself. 'I am immortal. For four thousand years I have waited to return to Earth, and you will not stop me.'

'Ah, shuddup,' said the werewolf as he swung the sword. The blade hit Teague's neck at the exact moment I pulled the metaphysical pin on my spell and exploded every cell in Teague's body.

Time seemed to stand still; energy exploded outwards like a bomb going off, the effect far greater than I could have caused with my spell. I could see the werewolf's swing pass through the point where Teague's neck should have been, but it had no substance now. Hitting nothing threw the werewolf off balance just as the outrushing blast of energy threw him across the room like a kite in a storm.

He smashed into a wall, leaving a dent, and I took all that in as the wash of energy hit me, lifting me off my feet in a violent surge. I tumbled, unsure which was way up, but I could feel the energy coursing through me. My synapses were on fire; my brain electrified as the energy tried to find a home within me. It seemed confused, like it was searching for its owner but couldn't find a way to get there.

A voice echoed in my head, but I couldn't understand the words. All I felt was confusion until I finally stopped tumbling because a wall got in the way. I slammed into it, my head, my right shoulder, my right hip, all making contact at the same time. I knew I was still alive because I was in so much pain.

My eyes were open, so I could see the red arcs of energy dancing over my skin.

I looked up when movement caught my eye; the werewolf staggered through the doorway from the hall, using the wall to keep himself upright. On him I could see the same energy crackling and fizzing over his skin, looking like it was going in and coming out again.

'I feel terrible,' he wheezed, holding himself upright by hanging on the doorframe.

In the hallway behind him, a form was taking shape, and it proved one thing: demons were immortal. The exploded cells from Teague's body were knitting back together. It sounded impossible in my head, but he was reforming in front of our eyes.

Between his slowly reforming body and where the werewolf hung on the doorframe, a head appeared, quickly followed by another. It was Heike and Katja coming up from the basement. 'I found a key,' she said. Then she got a proper look at us. 'Are you guys okay?' asked Heike.

'Oh yeah, just chipper,' said the werewolf. 'I was just thinking I might head to the gym, I feel so good.'

'You know you're glowing, right?' she asked.

I flailed an arm. 'I might need a hand to get up.'

She came into the hall, pulling Katja behind her, the young woman holding Heike's hand like it was a lifeline.

As she offered me a hand to pull myself upright, the werewolf behind her started to shrink. 'I don't think I can hold that form any longer,' he said. 'I don't feel so good.'

'Oh,' said Heike, turning her head to find herself confronted by a tall, well-hung, naked man. 'That was unexpected. Silly question,' she started, trying to focus on me but finding herself drawn to look at the naked former werewolf again. 'Shouldn't we be leaving now?'

Wearily, I nodded. 'Yes, very much so. I still can't open a portal, though. We need to find a shilt or some other creature that can do it for us. Then, having found them, I have to fight them and beat them but I have to beat them in such a way that there is enough of them left to open the portal so we can go through.'

Heike looked at me as I swayed on the spot like a drunk person. 'Are you up to that?'

I shrugged. 'Do I have a choice?'

'I will take you home,' said a new voice and I looked beyond the still reforming figure of Teague the demon to see a familiar face walking toward me. It was the man with the blue eyes.

Chapter 26

It was him.

The man with the blue eyes. The man from my kitchen. A cloud of rage descended even though I knew I had no energy left to deal with him.

'You,' I growled. 'You were in my house. You hurt my wife.'

He gave me his attention, levelling his eyes directly at mine. 'I am not responsible for what happened to your wife,' he replied, walking into the room past the werewolf with a casual manner.

Katja cowered behind Heike as the pair of them backed away.

I had a truckload of questions, but I was barely able to stand, and he got in first. 'I assume it was you who killed Edward earlier, yes?'

'He had it coming,' I managed to snarl.

Daniel looked away and tilted his head as if pondering the point. 'Perhaps from your perspective. But he was a useful tool to me. Someone I could outsource tasks to and expect them to be completed. He was part of my plan.'

'What plan?' I snapped.

He flipped his eyebrows and stopped moving. 'The plan that you will now be helping me to enact, dear fellow. Otto Schneider, isn't it? I claim you as my new familiar.' He indicated around the house. 'You clearly have some power.'

'How about if I unscrew your head like the last guy?' asked the werewolf, taking a step away from the door.

Daniel spun and crouched, twin orbs of dark red energy leaping into his palms and from them to blast the werewolf off his feet. He slammed into the door and fell to the floor. 'You, I have no use for at all,' Daniel said, standing up again.

I was drawing line energy in to feed my own spell. I didn't think I could win this time, but I saw no option but to fight until I was dead.

Daniel waggled a finger at me. 'I meant what I said. I will send you home now. All three of you.'

'Four,' I countered.

He raised an eyebrow. 'I just killed your friend the shapeshifter. No human can survive hellfire, even one possessing supernatural power. You can have the girl back. Return her to her parents. She was a prize worth taking, but I give respect where it is due. You fought well, and it was not only brave coming here to rescue her, but ingenious too. You can tell me how you achieved it later. You have one week to get your affairs on Earth in order. Then you belong to me.'

'And if I refuse to agree to this bargain?' I asked, my attention on the werewolf because I would swear I just saw his hand move.

'Then you stay here, and I don't send any of you home. The woman,' he raised his left hand, palm out with a fresh orb of death pointing straight into Heike's face, 'is of no interest. She possesses not the slightest modicum of magical ability, so I can kill her now. I believe Edward only snatched her because he thought I might be able to use you. Familiars bring status, you see. We all used to have them, several millennia ago before the realms were fractured. Now that the death curse is weakening, we are able to cross over more and more, bringing back those who appear to have some ability. I specialise in supplying the finest quality familiars.' He waved a dismissive hand. 'This is all detail you don't need to know yet. I can explain it all when you return.' He fixed me with an even gaze. 'So, which is it to be, Otto? I will send the three of you home, and I will ensure that no further shilt visit Bremen. This will disappoint many, but it is my pledge to you, something to … sweeten the deal, shall we say. However, you must agree to return in one week. I will come for you. If you resist, I will tear Bremen apart.'

I had no choice, and he knew it. However, he didn't know that the werewolf was getting up again. We could attack, maybe we could even find a way to win, but then what? We would still be trapped here and even if we then found a shilt and escaped this place, returning to the mortal realm, wouldn't Daniel just follow us and start the nightmare again? After all, he was immortal.

Just as Daniel sensed the movement behind him and spun around. I held up my hands to stop anything from happening. 'Stop.' My shout was aimed at the werewolf, his surprised face asking why I wanted to give in.

'I accept.' My voice was quiet as I said the words, but I had hope. Maybe he would undo whatever he had done to my wife. Maybe I could learn more and find a way to protect the people of Earth. There were a lot of maybes, but one thing was for sure: I had no choice.

Heike argued, 'You can't do that.'

'Yes, he can,' said Katja, clearly desperate to grasp the offer of being sent home and being released. I couldn't blame her; she had her whole life waiting for her.

Daniel nodded and opened a portal. Then he held up a finger to stop me. 'Otto, you have to agree to the binding.'

I squared myself to him, the word he used striking a dangerous chord. 'Binding?'

'Yes, Otto. You will bind yourself to me, or there is no deal.'

I knew I had no choice. The portal hung behind him like a glittering beacon of hope, but he could snap it shut in a second. 'What do I have to do?'

'A simple blood bond, nothing more. With that, you are bound to me and what we have agreed is indisputable.' He drew what looked like a large pin from a pocket. He gestured for me to step forward, and when I did, he held out his hand for me to put mine in his.

Without speaking, he took my right hand and pricked the thumb, then pressed it to his chest. The instant it made contact, I felt a tug deep within as if something had rebalanced, and a spark of energy on my thumb. I yanked it away to find that a print remained on Daniel's chest.

Right above his left pectoral was a thumbprint etched in fine detail.

As he buttoned up his shirt again, Daniel looked down at the new mark, inspecting it critically. Then he brought his eye up to meet mine. 'One week, Otto. I will come for you.'

My head was bowed in shame at having been beaten, but it was still the best result I could have hoped for. Stopping in front of him, I said, 'I want to know what happened to my wife.'

Daniel nodded as if considering my demand. 'When you return, I will explain.'

'I want to know now,' I growled, wondering if I should just punch him.

A flicker of hellfire crackled down his right arm in warning. 'Do not test me, wizard. My generosity can soon be rescinded.'

'Let's go,' I managed to murmur, touching Heike's arm to get her moving and nodding my head at the werewolf so he would do the same.

Daniel inspected him critically as he passed him to get to the portal. 'I believe you and I will meet again, Zachary Barnabus. You should be dead. That you are not is disturbing.'

The werewolf threw his arms up in frustration. 'You just told him my name, you dick.' Then he touched Daniel's arm and jumped through the portal without another word where he joined the two women. He was still naked and was standing in fifty millimetres of snow that was still falling. It had to have started recently because there was none of it when we sent the group home earlier.

I could see Bremen on the other side of the portal, the gap between the realms no more than two steps from my current position. My hometown stretched out before me, inviting even though it was cold, but all I had was a week. I wondered what I could do with it. I stepped through and felt the wave of cold air hit my exposed skin. It was a sweet feeling.

With an almost inaudible pop, the portal closed behind me, and the countdown to my surrender began.

Heike held out a hand for me to take. 'It's too cold to hang around, Otto. We need to get Katja home.'

Chapter 27

Kerstin's car was still parked where I left it outside Heike's house. It had a thick covering of snow now, but it was unmolested, the swords and other items I packed in preparation for what was to come still sitting in the passenger's footwell. I smiled to myself at the irony of it; how I managed anyway without the things I would normally have. I lost my wand when the task force buttheads tasered and imprisoned me and took my defensive ring. Both losses made me stronger; being forced to manage without them was the best thing that could have happened to me.

'Are you coming in?' asked Heike, pausing in the street on her way to her door.

I thought about it for a second, but I wanted to go home. Actually, what I wanted to do was go to the hospital to visit Kerstin, but it was the middle of the night and way after visiting hours. Three days since I saw her, the longest I had ever gone. I shook my head as I started to sweep the snow from Kerstin's car. It was fresh, so hadn't stuck and came off easily.

She twitched, turning toward her house, where she was clearly desperate to go, and then swivelled back to face me as her indecision finally chose a course of action.

She walked back to me in the road, placing a hand on my arm to stop what I was doing. 'Thank you, Otto. You came for me. I wouldn't be coming home to my children if it wasn't for you.'

I shrugged. I wanted to say something in response, but the words wouldn't come.

'We can work out a way to beat him. We'll meet tomorrow when we have slept and can think straight. There will be a way to prevent him from taking you.'

I shrugged again. I didn't think we would, but I didn't want to tell her that. She needed to go inside and be with her family right now. To get her moving, I said, 'Go, Heike. Your husband will be overwhelmed with relief to see you. I'm sure the last two days have been hell for him.'

'Only because he had to deal with the kids all by himself,' she joked. She patted my arm though and left me, heading back to her house, her steps quick in her desperation to get there.

The car started on the first turn of the key, and I patted its dashboard in thank you to whatever car god was out there watching over lonely men out on freezing nights.

Getting home didn't take long; the streets were empty, and I finally had a clock to look at. It was quarter to five in the morning. During the drive, I thought about the look Herr Weber gave me when we returned his daughter.

Katja had run up her driveway, Heike and I taking it more slowly in the snow, but her fifteen-year-old sense of danger had no concern for the possibility of slipping over and hurting herself. By the time we arrived at the elevated front door, her insistent hammering and shouting had woken her parents, the door being flung open just as we caught up to her.

Her mother had collapsed as Katja clamped onto her, the two ending up on their knees on the floor of their lobby.

'Did you catch the man who took her?' Herr Weber demanded to know. 'Is he in custody?'

I replied, 'Not exactly.'

He glanced from me to Heike, back to me and then to Heike again. 'What does that mean? Did you arrest him? Is he dead?'

Heike stepped into the house. 'I think it would be best if Katja explained.'

Katja broke away from her mother, standing up but keeping hold of her mother's hand as she looked at her father. It was clear the relationship she had with her father was vastly different from the one she had with her mother. She had been missing for two days, but he hadn't even hugged her yet. Looking at her father rather than us, she said, 'I can take it from here.' She looked back over her shoulder to make eye contact with Heike and me. 'You two both have homes to go to. I'm safe now.'

I nodded. I felt confident she was indeed safe. As we backed away, Herr Weber shouted after us, 'You're leaving? What is this?'

Katja tried to stop him. 'Daddy.'

'No. They have a responsibility to tell me what is going on. I want to know what happened to your kidnapper. Why was there no ransom note?' He stopped arguing with his daughter and addressed us directly. 'Stop right there!' I raised an eyebrow, but Heike just kept on walking, uncertain whether she would even be a police officer tomorrow. 'Come back here and answer my questions.'

'Daddy!'

'Be quiet, Katja, I'll deal with you later.'

Herr Weber wasn't used to being defied and looked satisfied when I went back toward him. I was feeling punchy; the events of the last week combined with fatigue and the threat of captivity and enslavement to come eroding all my barriers as I pulled ley line energy in and raised my hands. I went up the steps with a spell forming in my right hand. It was air that I was conjuring, I wanted to scare him, not hurt him, but in the end, I achieved both.

'Your daughter was taken by a demon,' I roared as I used the air spell to lift him from the floor. 'She has been terrified and terrorised, and she is here because people stood up to get her back. If you ever try to order me to do anything again, I will show you just how little you know about the world around you.'

Herr Weber was a metre off the carpet and looked about ready to wet himself when I cut the spell and dumped him on his arse. He crashed to the floor and scrambled away, looking terrified. I left him there, striding back toward the door where Frau Weber and Katja were still holding hands.

Frau Weber's eyes held no fear when she looked at me, and Katja let go of her hand so she could stop me, throwing her arms around me to pin me in a hug that was more for her benefit than mine.

Their door closed behind me as I went down the steps.

'Feel better?' Heike asked, her face telling me my outburst and display of magic hadn't been the best idea ever.

I smiled to myself now as I remembered it, pushing my front door open and finally finding myself back home.

There was a man on my couch.

Chapter 28

I recognised him as the second in command of the task force from Berlin, though I was quite certain that whatever they were, they were not a special branch of the police.

I drew in some ley line energy, conjuring a spell even though I was now in my own home and would end up wrecking it.

He lifted both of his hands to show he was alone and not holding a weapon. I closed and opened my eyes to look around with my second sight. He was human, I could tell that much, and there were no supernatural creatures anywhere nearby.

'Deputy Commissioner Schmidt has been replaced,' he announced calmly.

I kept the spell in my hand. 'By you?'

He nodded. 'I am, as of about twelve hours ago, Deputy Commissioner Rudi Bliebtreu. I wish to apologise on behalf of the Supernatural Investigation Alliance for your treatment, about your illegal detainment and incarceration at the facility in Berlin. I came in person in the hope that you might believe that I am sincere and that you might listen to a proposal.'

I sat opposite him, resting my weary body on my couch. He had given me his real name, and that bought him a few more seconds' grace. 'You thought it acceptable to break into my house in your bid to gain my trust?'

My question didn't even make him blink. 'I thought it better than waiting outside where I might draw attention to myself.'

'You just called your operation the Alliance,' I pointed out, changing the subject. 'I thought you were a police task force.'

He sat forward on the couch, looking directly at me. 'That was a perfectly good pretence and will be maintained for the general populace. You are not part of the general population though, are you, Herr Schneider? You are something else entirely.' I didn't know if he was expecting me to reply, but I didn't, and there was a beat of silence before he continued speaking. 'The Alliance was set up to investigate, define, and ultimately tackle the growing supernatural problem. Instances of people being taken is on the increase. Reports of unexplained events have risen starkly in the last fifty years which had caused research into human history. As far back as records go, reliable records, that is, there have been tales of demons, of witches, of blood-sucking supernatural creatures. It is written off as legend or folk tale by everyone, but I suspect you will be able to tell me a different story, Herr Schneider.'

'Why are you here?' I asked, trying to get him to the point so I could get a shower and get to bed. 'Specifically, why are you here in my house at this time?'

'Several citizens returned to Bremen a few hours ago. They had been missing for different periods of time, but all claimed to have been taken by a wizard called Edward Blake and a demon known as Daniel. They also claimed that you killed Edward Blake and were on your way to rescue a girl.' I didn't say anything. 'Shall I assume that you were successful in your quest?'

I pursed my lips, thinking about what I wanted to admit to a man running a clandestine organisation specifically interested in persons with supernatural abilities. 'I was.'

'So Katja Weber is back with her parents?'

I nodded. 'I believe the immediate danger in Bremen has passed.'

He inclined his head, squinting his eyes a little as he attempted to decipher my words. 'Why do you say that?'

'I made a pact, of sorts. The shilt, those nasty creatures who are responsible for the recent deaths, will not be returning any time soon.' Now I had a question for him. 'Tell, me Bliebtreu, what is it that the Alliance is attempting to achieve?'

'The leaders within my organisation believe the Earth is heading toward a cataclysmic event. The increase of recorded incidents, of creatures attacking and killing like the recent spree here in Bremen, of people being taken from their homes in front of their loved ones by a person who vanishes through a vertical wall of iridescent air, can all be mathematically tracked, plotted, and extrapolated. If they continue unabated, the Earth will be awash with events in less than twenty years.' Schmidt had told me as much while I was in my cell.

I had a question. 'Why was Schmidt replaced?'

I listened intently to see if Bliebtreu would lie. 'He was taking human supernaturals captive. That is expressly against policy. He intended to experiment on you. Once I discovered why he ordered your arrest, I intervened.'

'Okay,' I replied, accepting what he said and moving on. 'You said something about a proposal.'

He exhaled through his nose, an outrushing air sound that could mean a thousand different things. 'I want you to join us.'

I laughed. I couldn't stop it from escaping my lips.

'Humanity is going to need people like you, Herr Schneider. People who can stand up to fight where others cannot. This war will be fought by a very different type of soldier…'

I held up my hand to stop him. 'I'm afraid I will not be available. You can save your breath from the big speech. It's not that it won't work, which,' I chuckled again, 'it probably wouldn't, but I am genuinely not going to be available.'

Bliebtreu sighed. 'That is disappointing, Herr Schneider. I had hoped you might see that we need you. There are others; I am gathering a team, as many people as I can find with the ability to do what others cannot. Our reach is spreading; more and more countries sign on each month which is why we call ourselves The Alliance: we are an alliance of nations.'

'As I said. It doesn't matter if I want to join your club or not. I will not be available.' A voice echoed in my head to remind me I had less than seven days now. 'I've no wish to be rude, Herr Bliebtreu, but I have had rather a tiring few days, and I would really like to get some sleep. I'm sure you can let yourself out since you so deftly let yourself in.'

He nodded, standing up and slipping his winter coat back on. Then he took out a card and placed it on the low coffee table between us, pushing it across the surface so I could see it. 'If you change your mind...' Then he made to leave but paused just as he was about to start walking. 'There was another man in the cells in Berlin with you. His name was Zachary Barnabus. I saw the footage of the two of you escaping. Do you happen to know his current whereabouts?'

Epilogue: The Shifter

Arriving in the snowy streets of Bremen, there were four of us in the street. Three of them with very specific places to go, unlike me, who had nowhere to go at all. Heike looked at Otto and held out her hand to get him moving. 'It's too cold to hang around Otto,' she said. 'We need to get Katja home.'

He nodded, offering no argument. There was a train station not far away where they would find a taxi, no doubt. I didn't follow them, weighing up my options, but Otto noticed, turning back to frown at me curiously. 'Not coming?'

I shook my head; slowly back and forth to say no. 'I think I should move on. This feels complete. You can take the girl home. You don't need me anymore. Besides, I don't do well in built-up areas: too many people, too likely to lose my temper and hurt someone. I avoid cities if I can.' It was the truth, something I avoided telling people as a principle. I trusted Otto though I couldn't tell you why; there was just something about him. Cities were bad news for me, that was something I knew for certain. Being near people, in general, was a recipe for aggravation, and I was too efficient at hurting people and always too filled with remorse afterward to put myself in that position if I didn't have to.

Softly, Otto asked Heike, 'Can you wait a moment?' Then he jogged back to me. 'Are you sure? You're butt naked in the snow on a winter's night in North Germany. You can move on in the morning if you don't want to stay. Do you even have anywhere to go?'

'There's always somewhere to go,' I replied. 'Besides, I don't feel the cold. I guess it's a shapeshifter thing.' Offering him a moment of seriousness, I said, 'There's at least one warrant out for my arrest, and I don't think those dicks from the Alliance will just decide to leave me alone now. Staying here will just bring heat to you, and your friend over there is a cop. I'm gonna split; there's people out there who might need my help. Good luck with the demon.'

Then we shook hands. It felt like the right thing to do. I didn't know if I had ever really had a friend; I was quite distrustful of people in general, but Otto came somewhere close.

I watched from a corner as he and the two ladies were eaten up by the swirling snow, then I turned and started running. I would find clothes, I always had before, and I would find someplace to be; someplace where someone needed me.

The End

Author Note:

Hi there,

If you have read this far, then well done. I always read the author notes, but then... I'm an author. I write because I absolutely have to. I won my first award when aged just ten but didn't pursue it as a career as you might expect. Three decades went by before I knuckled down to write what became my first novel, most of the years eaten up by a long career in the army.

I get awoken in the night by story ideas, or by the thoughts of my characters as they wake me up to tell me something. Often, they point out something I have forgotten, so they are quite useful. Other times they want me to stop throwing them into dire peril and wake me to complain. I also have a retired police dog in one of my series and he likes to wake me up because he is a dick head.

I first conceived this series as a story about a soldier. Wounded on operations somewhere, he awoke to find a piece of shrapnel in his head had awoken certain powers. That idea stewed for more than a year, growing arms and legs and getting bigger and bigger. Now, what I have is four series set within the same universe. The False Gods are returning to Earth and they will bring destruction with them. The separate series will intertwine and overlap and then converge to give you a final battle.

I am very excited by the opportunity to write it.

UNTETHERED MAGIC

There is an important part for you to play in my fantasies though; none of what I do means anything if no one reads it. My characters only truly have life when you form them in your imagination. I will do my best to paint the picture, to show you what I see, but their adventures take place in your minds as my words play out for you.

For that, in advance, I thank you.

Steve Higgs

Eccles, Kent

February 2020

More Books By Steve Higgs

Blue Moon Investigations
Paranormal Nonsense
The Phantom of Barker Mill
Amanda Harper Paranormal Detective
The Klowns of Kent
Dead Pirates of Cawsand
In the Doodoo With Voodoo
The Witches of East Malling
Crop Circles, Cows and Crazy Aliens
Whispers in the Rigging
Bloodlust Blonde – a short story
Paws of the Yeti
Under a Blue Moon – A Paranormal Detective Origin Story
Night Work
Lord Hale's Monster
The Herne Bay Howlers
Undead Incorporated
The Ghoul of Christmas Past
The Sandman
Jailhouse Golem
Shadow in the Mine
Ghost Writer

Felicity Philips Investigates
To Love and to Perish
Tying the Noose
Aisle Kill Him
A Dress to Die For
Wedding Ceremony Woes

Patricia Fisher Cruise Mysteries
The Missing Sapphire of Zangrabar
The Kidnapped Bride
The Director's Cut
The Couple in Cabin 2124
Doctor Death
Murder on the Dancefloor
Mission for the Maharaja
A Sleuth and her Dachshund in Athens
The Maltese Parrot
No Place Like Home

Patricia Fisher Mystery Adventures
What Sam Knew
Solstice Goat
Recipe for Murder
A Banshee and a Bookshop
Diamonds, Dinner Jackets, and Death
Frozen Vengeance
Mug Shot
The Godmother
Murder is an Artform
Wonderful Weddings and Deadly Divorces
Dangerous Creatures

Patricia Fisher: Ship's Detective Series
The Ship's Detective
Fitness Can Kill
Death by Pirates
First Dig Two Graves

Albert Smith Culinary Capers
Pork Pie Pandemonium
Bakewell Tart Bludgeoning
Stilton Slaughter
Bedfordshire Clanger Calamity
Death of a Yorkshire Pudding
Cumberland Sausage Shocker
Arbroath Smokie Slaying
Dundee Cake Dispatch
Lancashire Hotpot Peril
Blackpool Rock Bloodshed
Kent Coast Oyster Obliteration
Eton Mess Massacre
Cornish Pasty Conspiracy

Realm of False Gods
Untethered magic
Unleashed Magic
Early Shift
Damaged but Powerful
Demon Bound
Familiar Territory
The Armour of God
Live and Die by Magic
Terrible Secrets

About the Author

At school, the author was mostly disinterested in every subject except creative writing, for which, at age ten, he won his first award. However, calling it his first award suggests that there have been more, which there have not. Accolades may come but, in the meantime, he is having a ball writing mystery stories and crime thrillers and claims to have more than a hundred books forming an unruly queue in his head as they clamour to get out. He lives in the south-east corner of England with a duo of lazy sausage dogs. Surrounded by rolling hills, brooding castles, and vineyards, he doubts he will ever leave, the beer is just too good.

If you are a social media fan, you should copy the link below into your browser to join my very active Facebook group. You'll find a host of friends waiting there, some of whom have been with me from the very start.

My Facebook group get first notification when I publish anything new, plus cover reveals and free short stories, but more than that, they all interact with each other, sharing inside jokes, and answering question.

f   facebook.com/stevehiggsauthor

You can also keep updated with my books via my website:

https://stevehiggsbooks.com/

Printed in Great Britain
by Amazon